BEYOND THE WILDS

Steve + Nadya,

Hope you enjoy the reading
of this novel as much as I
enjoyed the writing.

Love
Mary

BEYOND THE WILDS

Helena's Pursuit of Freedom

Mary Kolisnyk Spry-Myers

This is a work of fiction. Names, characters, places and incidents
either are the product of the author's imagination or are used fictitiously,
and any resemblance to any actual persons, living or dead, events, or
locales is entirely coincidental.

To order additional copies of this book, contact:
Xlibris Corporation
1-888-795-4274
www.Xlibris.com
Orders@Xlibris.com
17605

CONTENTS

DEDICATION

This book is dedicated to my parents and
grandparents, now deceased, to my husband
Gordon, son Ranny, daughter Denise
and husband Ron, granddaughters Megan and
Nicole, and all family members.
I would like to express my very special thanks
to all who assisted me and gave so generously
of their time. It is my hope that readers
will enjoy the story, including the historical
component. I hope readers of Ukrainian
and other origins will be inspired in developing
their knowledge of their family,
culture and heritage.

FOREWORD

Changes in our life
   Are challenges of progression
   Each experience leaves us
      With many personal thoughts
      To ponder and reminisce.

We do not know our future
   How our cards may play
   We must prepare ourselves
      For the unexpected, the unknown
      Feelings may vary from happy to sad.

I n the 1800s, a large number of the European population migrated to Canada. One of these immigrants had the strong desire and challenge to gain freedom from his dominant, uncaring landlord in Ukraine. He opted for a new life—a new country for himself and his family—in the wilds of Canada. Agents from Manitoba, Canada, promised the immigrants ownership of large parcels of land (160 acres) for only ten dollars. The very primitive lifestyle in the wild, wooded area of this new country provided unbelievable experiences to this family's survival and adjustment. This family saga continues in the life of the eldest child, Michael, his wife, and children. It tells a human story that is embedded in history, highlighting the courage and strength of one particular individual, Helena. The story takes you on many interesting journeys across the sea, through time, to a conclusion.

Other works of Mary Kolisnyk Spry-Myers:

1) Children's Book—A Hole in the Sky
   Published by Dorrance Publishing Co
2) Cassette of Poems with Background Music
   A Reflection of Life's Seasons
   Music by Doug Campbell

This work of historical fiction is educational.

SELECTED BIBLIOGRAPHY

The Ukrainians in Canada
O.W.Gerus and J.E.Red
Department of History
University Of Manitoba, Canada

To the Promised Land
Contributions of Ukrainian Immigrants and
Their Descendents to Canadian Society

Canadian Culture Series No. 3

MY COUNTRY

My ancestors toiled as homesteaders
On arrival in this great land
They persevered through hardships
Without receiving a helping hand
My country gained from this action
Inherent in population growth
Families grew as they multiplied
Following each marriage oath

My country glows in the darkness
My country shines in the light
My ancestors achieved in this country
They toiled from morning til night

The potential in my great country
With water, land, food, and dignity
Reflects much growth and happiness
From pursuing each opportunity
Risks and challenges are open
To all who plan a life so divine
Freedom, education, health care
Such a virtue, this country of mine

My country glows in the darkness
My country shines in the light
Feelings of warmth and security
Remain with me from morning til night

PART ONE
FROM UKRAINE TO THE CANADIAN WILDS

WORKING ON THE RAILROAD

WORKING ON THE RAILROAD

ONE

It was a beautiful, warm, sunny day in Naples, Florida, with just a few clouds hovering in the sky, providing a very acceptable and comfortable temperature during the middle of the month of February. Emily was traveling to Canada, dressed in warm clothing, much too warm for southern temperatures. She had prepared herself for the bitter cold when arriving in the Northwest later that day. Emily had spent many years in Canada as a child, wife and mother, plus as full-time employee in a large hospital. Following retirement in 1989, Emily and her husband, Peter, spent the winters in Naples. They enjoyed their home on the beach and the comforts of warm temperature, no snow to shovel, and no frost or ice to contend with. But now, before one of these winters was over, Emily had to fly to her homeland in Canada to attend the funeral of her mother, Helena.

Helena's health had taken a gradual decline, becoming a problem during the last few years. She had developed diabetes late in her life and had difficulty adjusting to the appropriate diet. Desserts stood prominently in her lifestyle, as she loved preparing them for her family and friends. She also took delight in eating them, along with a cup of tea in mid-mornings, mid-afternoons, and evenings. Helena believed desserts pose no great harm to her body if she ate them, provided she had taken her insulin. She clung tightly to this belief, even though her family and health care workers frequently tried to change her mind and attitude.

It was extremely difficult for Emily to accept the fact that Helena would not be with them in person anymore. Helena had made her final departure from family and friends. She was loved by so many, but not one person was able to improve her health and prolong her life.

Many thoughts and memories surfaced during the last twenty-four hours while Emily was packing and preparing herself for the inevitable event, her mother's funeral. Her most vivid memory was of the inability of her mother to continue caring for her husband, Michael, and herself in their own home. Helena had always functioned as a very strong, independent person, and having to be cared for by others was not easily acceptable to her. She wanted so much to continue shopping, preparing food, having food available to serve to family and friends everytime they visited her. This had been an important part of Helena's life and she became frustrated and depressed when it couldn't continue.

Emily had many questions about herself that remained unanswered as she quietly placed her packed luggage down at the bedroom door and sat down on the bed for a few minutes. How does one say goodbye to a mother who has been so instrumental in guiding you to a life of richness and fulfillment? When the love you shared has remained with you and you do not want it to end? What feelings will I have after the funeral? She gave me so much over the years. Did she really know how much I appreciated and loved her? The death of Emily's father, Michael, fourteen months earlier seemed easier to handle as her mother remained with them. During time spent together following Michael's death, they discussed some of their past family experiences and activities, sharing many happy memories.

Visualizing the change in Emily's life without her mother brought tears flowing down her cheeks. Even though they lived miles apart, Emily always experienced strong feelings of caring and support from her mother. These feelings provided her with inspiration during her most overwhelming endeavors, including her career and motherhood. Maybe these feelings will always be a part of me, thought Emily as she reached for her luggage and walked out the door to join her husband, Peter.

During the trip to the airport, Peter and their friend, Mark, who was commuting to the airport with Emily and Peter, took up most of the conversation. Mark was excited about changing his return airline ticket, extending his vacation to four more days of sun, fun and time on the beach. He was very chatty. Emily was very much absorbed in her own thoughts, not fully aware of the conversation taking place between the two men. She was looking forward to some quiet time alone at the airport and in-flight. As Emily embraced Peter at the airport before leaving, she experienced a more relaxed feeling, stimulated by a surge of energy. She could feel Helena's spirit close to her, guiding her in this voyage. You have always been my guardian angel, Mom, she said to herself, as she headed toward the check-in area for Minneapolis-bound passengers.

After buckling herself in her seat, Emily felt secure as though she was flying to visit her parents on one of her planned vacations. I just want to keep on flying, she said to herself as the miles kept adding up. The low, humming sound of the airplane gave her a sense of peacefulness. She closed her eyes and thought about the happy get-togethers her family members had had at her parents' home, eating, talking, laughing, and playing jokes on one another. They were pleasant memories and she was sorry to have them interrupted by a flight attendant who placed a lunch tray on the table in front of her and another flight attendant who asked "tea or coffee?"

Food was not a priority for Emily at this time and she did not feel hungry. She picked away at her salad with her thoughts focused on meeting her sister, Sophie, in Minneapolis. Sophie was flying from Los Angeles and they would meet in Minneapolis, and travel the remainder of the journey together. For some reason it was most reassuring, thinking about traveling together. They would be able to give each other some support.

Lunch was over. Flight attendants were serving drinks and peanuts as the movie with Sally Field and Robin Williams was shown on the screen, creating much laughter from the passengers. Emily tried to concentrate on the movie, but her parents' lives kept flashing in front of her—the memories of her father and mother she herself remembered, and memories narrated by her parents and grandparents. At one time, Emily had a very strong desire to travel to Ukraine with her parents for a visit to their birth land, plus any relatives in that area. After many discussions on this subject, her parents decided their memories were a great part of re-living the past, and they did not wish them obscured with change. They chose not to visit Ukraine.

Suddenly, Emily felt as though her parents wanted to share their experiences with her again, as they had done so many times over the years. She made herself comfortable by putting her seat back and reclining quietly with her eyes closed, concentrating and visualizing her parents as children in the village of Zelisia, in the province of Galicia in Western Ukraine. Emily's parents were born in this village in the early 1900s. They immigrated to Canada with her grandparents at a young age. Helena was much younger than Michael when she arrived in Canada. Her memories of Ukraine were more limited than Michael's. Emily loved to escape into fantasy with her grandparents and parents, into their past lives, a long time ago. Emily also thought about her life with her parents, their unbelievable strength in following their dreams—so many fond memories.

TWO

U kraine is situated in South eastern Europe, extending to the Don River on the east, Caucasus Mountains and Black Sea on the south, Romania and Czechoslovakia on the southwest, Poland on the west and Russia on the northeast. The Carpathian Mountains border Zelisia to the west, separating them from the rest of Europe. Lviv stands out as the nearest largest city, situated in the north. The Black Sea is approximately three hundred miles south of Zelisia. Emily's grandparents had longed to visit the Black Sea area but left Ukraine without having this opportunity.

Ukraine is about one-tenth the size of Canada. It is approximately one thousand miles in the east-west direction and approximately five hundred miles in the north-south direction.

The countryside of Ukraine is very picturesque with many contrasts: deep flowing rivers, winding lakes, lush green woods, fruit groves, crystal-clear lakes, beautiful mountains, sunny coasts, fertile soil and flat land rich in natural resources.

Although male Ukrainian peasants had been freed from serfdom in 1848, and were now being allowed to own real estate property, they were too impoverished to purchase land. They worked with very primitive equipment in the fields and gardens of their landlord in most days, from morning until night. During the harvest season a sickle or scythe was used to cut down the stalks of the grain. A sickle is an oval piece of steel as thick as a butcher knife, narrower and sharper, with a wooden handle. A scythe is much larger than the sickle, with less curvature. The sheaves were pounded with a flail, a manual-threshing device, consisting of a long wooden handle and a shorter, free-swinging stick attached to its end. This separated the straw from the kernels. Peasants received one sheaf of grain (a bundle of stalks) out of seven they cut. That was to be their wage from their landlord

Peasants had to pay their landlord for trees they cut down for their own use and for pasturing their cows and sheep on the landlord's property. If unable to pay, the children attended the herds along the roadway. Most men worked in France or Germany to save money for a cow and a small acreage of land.

The climate in Ukraine is similar to certain areas of Canada and United States, buried in deep snow in the winter, with frosty days and nights. Winters begin at around Christmas, lasting approximately two to three months. Agricultural work in the fields begins in early March. The climate is conducive to growing fruits and vegetables.

Abundantly rich, agricultural land, plus a moderate climate gave Ukraine a reputation as the "breadbasket" of Europe. This natural resource lacked geographical barriers against powerful outsiders. Thus, Ukraine was an easy prey to invaders from all directions. Ukraine has been conquered and partitioned by various alien powers. Neighboring countries, mainly Russia, Poland, and Austria, have also dominated certain parts of its land. After the assimilation of most of its aristocracy by Poland and Russia, the peasants were the remaining people who stuck with the Ukrainian language and national traditions, and made a living from farming. Working close to the earth and natural elements was reflected in their language and literature, habits and customs, religious life, music, art and philosophy.

Western Ukraine, consisting of the provinces of Galicia, Bukovyna and Trans-carpathia was part of the Austro-Hungarian empire. In Galicia, the Polish gentry and Polonized Ukrainians formed the ruling class. Religious affiliation provided a means of national identification. The Ukrainians were members of the Greek Catholic Church and adhered to Ukrainian traditions, including the use of the Slavonic language and a married parish clergy. The Poles were staunch Roman Catholics and they regarded Ukrainian conversion to Roman Catholicism as acceptance of Polish nationality. In Bukovyna, although the Ukrainians and Romanians belonged to the Orthodox Church, the Romanian gentry dominated politics and the economy in the region.

THREE

M ichael was out of breath when he arrived at his favorite swimming hole. Still panting from the quarter-mile run just completed, he quickly disrobed, except for his under shorts, jumped into the clear, blue water, swam a few strokes, then turned onto his back to relax and ponder the thoughts troubling him that day. Michael felt extremely listless, as he had not slept much the previous night. He kept thinking of the reason he could not sleep.

After falling asleep next to his brother, John, on the mattress in the large family room, Michael was suddenly woken by loud voices which he immediately realized were his parents'. They were discussing an offer and plans to immigrate to Canada. His father would be leaving first, traveling by steamship from Austria. His mother and children would remain until the garden was sold off, then take a long voyage by steamship to join his father. Michael had difficulty falling back to sleep after hearing the conversation in the next room. He tried to remember details about Canada from the geography classes at school, but all that entered his mind was a vision of a big country very far away. He felt frightened and insecure as he tossed and turned the rest of the night

Michael loved his homeland, Ukraine. The river close to their home provided a perfect escape zone for him as he lay on the bank following a swim, fantasizing about his future. The beautiful valley— engulfed with rows and rows of a large variety of fruit trees and the thick, green, sprawling meadows— was his domain.

When Michael swam and relaxed floating on his back in the river, he listened to the birds chirping and frolicking in the trees. He enjoyed this peaceful environment immensely, content and certain he did not want to leave it. However, thoughts of a new country offering more for his family and himself did stimulate some interest.

One of Michael's dreams was to become a large landowner in his homeland in Galicia and gain some economic control. The peasant life he and his family had experienced provided love and happiness, but there was no financial gain for them, no matter how hard they continued to work. The landowner took the profits reaped by his parents. Michael wanted an opportunity to upgrade himself to the status of a landowner in a few years, thus achieving a little wealth for his family.

In the past, Michael had heard his parents speak of the large number of peasants from Eastern Galicia who had immigrated to Brazil, attracted by offers of free acres of property and free passage. Letters received from many of these immigrants indicated they were having difficulty with a radically different climate, tropical diseases, hard labor on coffee plantations and unfair treatment. His parents had shown no interest in joining this group. Why would they be considering a move to Canada? Would living in Canada be an improvement to their present lifestyle and the experiences in Brazil?

At the age of twelve, being the eldest of five children, Michael's responsibilities included a number of chores. He attended to the cows and barn, cared for his two younger siblings when he was not at school and assisted his mother with the household chores. He enjoyed learning and reading very much, was a good student, and had made a good impression with the teacher, Mr. Harpik. Michael and his siblings studied both the Ukrainian and Polish languages.

While assisting Mr. Harpik between his classes the previous week, Michael noticed a beautiful girl, much younger than himself, sitting at the back of the classroom, reading. She looked up from her book just as Michael glanced at her. As their eyes met, the contact felt very special to Michael, producing an exciting feeling in his body. He shyly turned his head away wondering whether she had experienced a similar reaction. She is too young to feel the way I do, he thought to himself.

The days following were filled with visions of this girl, particularly as Michael relaxed while floating on his back in the river. He hoped to see her again and had decided he would build up enough courage to talk to her, should there be another opportunity. Relocating to another country would certainly put an end to any possible meeting. This upset Michael. He decided it was necessary to confront his parents regarding the conversation he overheard last night.

Michael came out of the water, lay in the sun on the bank of the river until his under shorts and body went partially dry, then quickly put on his trousers and shirt. He ran back to the house with his unbuttoned shirt flapping in the wind. Family members were sitting down to supper as Michael entered the family room. He sensed a very quiet atmosphere. Jacob appeared very happy as he sat down on his stool at the table. Mary appeared distressed and her eyes were puffy. She had her shawl placed over the left side of her face as she sat. This was very unusual, Michael thought. Had she been crying? He wondered if his mother was upset with the conversation that he partially heard last night. A good time for discussion, Michael thought to himself as he inhaled the aroma of freshly baked bread, which he loved so much.

FOUR

Jacob Karpiak, Michael's father, was a tall, handsome, slim man with dark brown wavy hair and hazel-colored eyes. He was very popular in the neighborhood, performing as a comedian, following a few drinks of alcohol. The alcohol was a home brew made by the men in the village. Jacob loved to tell funny stories to all age groups. He also entertained by playing the violin and sang in the male choir at the village Greek Catholic Church.

All family members were invited to the neighborhood get-togethers and they all made a point of attending as they looked forward to the peer interaction and socialization. It was important to their lifestyle. They danced together, performing the steps in spirited sequences. They sang happy songs to cheer them, and sang sad songs to remind them of their many dreary situations. Family members attended church, observing holy days. Each morning, everyone knelt in prayer before breakfast.

Mary Karpiak, Michael's mother, was average in height and weight, had straight dark brown hair pulled back and rolled in a bun. Occasionally, before going to bed at night, she let her hair down and wore it hanging to her waist. Mary wore a shawl on her head most of the time during the day. Her blouses had long sleeves and her skirts were ankle length with a fully gathered waist. Mary's beauty was overwhelming in her large, blue eyes. She enjoyed socializing but was a little shy and uncomfortable sitting around chatting. She expressed the need to be working at something, not wasting time. Mary brought her knitting or cross-stitch embroidery work to the get-togethers, utilizing the time more effectively, to her opinion. She was not used to sitting and relaxing empty—handed at home so she felt more comfortable knitting, mending, or embroidering when socializing in the neighborhood. Exchanging recipes, ideas in homemaking, family care, and gardening were very important to Mary. She had many creative ideas and was happy to share them with her lady friends and relatives. She was well respected in her neighborhood and a role model to many family members and friends.

John Karpiak, the second son of Jacob and Mary, was 11 months younger than his brother, Michael. He did not adapt to the school curriculum and activities as quickly as Michael, but enjoyed learning at a slower pace. He idolized his older brother. They had a close relationship. Hoeing and weeding the garden were John's regular chores. He would rush home after school and work in the garden until he was called to the house for supper. During the summer months, John accepted total responsibility for the garden, including sales at the market. He loved his mother very much and was aware of her difficulty during the recent pregnancy and delivery of Ann, the youngest child. John wanted to reduce her workload. Mary never complained about her health but appeared to be tired and more abrupt in dealing with the family in the past year. John shared these concerns regarding their mother with Michael and they both agreed to assist her as much as possible.

Jean Karpiak, the third child and now a happy-go-lucky 10-year-old, was named after her maternal grandmother. She did not physically resemble her grandmother, but according to her two older brothers, she had the same characteristics as her. Michael and John had noticed their grandmother slip away from helping out with routine duties whenever she could and when spending time with them. For example, she usually left the house to view the garden when it was time to clean up supper, arriving back in the house when the cleanup was completed or close to being done. She was very complimentary about the supper and garden.

They felt Jean did not carry her load in managing the family chores. After meals, she seemed to disappear from the house, leaving the boys with the dishes to clean up plus manage the two younger children. Michael felt he had a responsibility in discussing this issue with his sister but delayed the conversation. He did not want to create conflict in the home while his mother was getting her strength back from the birth of her last child, Ann.

Paul Karpiak, the fourth child, was a very active four-year-old with curly, fair hair and blue eyes. He loved his baby sister, Ann, and spent the day playing beside her, watching over her. Ann was six months old, a beautiful, chubby baby, very content to be propped up in her cradle for long periods, watching her brother as he entertained her.

FIVE

Family members worked together, with assistance from the neighbors, in building their house, barn, summer kitchen, outside toilet, and most of the furnishings. Mud and straw were used to make blocks. These blocks formed the structure of each home. They were covered with a clay paste. Limestone whitewash was painted over the clay, both in the interior and exterior of the home, providing a brighter, cheerier atmosphere. The roof consisted of many layers of straw.

These straw roofs functioned effectively during the winter months, but in the spring, the wind and rain played havoc with them, creating uncovered areas, causing rain to drip into the home. A few months after Ann was born, the rain was heavy, dripping into the home through many areas of the roof. Michael quickly moved Ann, in her cradle, underneath the table. It was a dry area as the table was covered with a piece of oilcloth. Michael kept Ann there until the rain stopped. The big job then was to repair the roof before the next rainfall. Michael and John worked together on this project quite frequently.

The family home consisted of two rooms, primitively furnished; there was no electrical service or running water. All of the water used in the home was carried up in pails from the river. When the river was flowing, the water was used for everything, including drinking water, and cooking. When the river was stagnant, the water used for drinking and cooking was boiled, and then cooled at room temperature. Mary laundered in the river, using a scrub board, and strong soap made of lye and fat, during the late spring, all summer, and early fall. Sunny days were chosen for this chore, if it was at all possible. During the remainder of the year, Mary did laundry in the home. The articles washed were all dried outside. Larger articles were placed on the fence and the smaller articles were hung on branches from the trees. In the wintertime, the clothing froze while hanging outside and would have to be brought in the house and spread around on the benches to complete the drying process. The house smelled so fresh during this drying period and the clothing remained fresh. Ironing was usually planned for the following day using the method of heating irons on the cook stove. Mary liked to bake bread the day she ironed as the stove was kept at a high temperature most of the day, heating the irons.

The floors in the home were built of wide strips of wood nailed down at each end. Mary was very particular about keeping the floors swept each day with a broom made from twigs and branches. A weekly chore was to get down on her hands and knees and scrub the floor, using a brush dipped in soap and water solution. Mary braided rugs in an oval design from strips of rags and scattered these rugs on the wood floor. These rugs provided warmth and comfort but were extremely cumbersome to launder and dry.

The beds, table, wooden benches, clay stoves, both inside and outside the home, were built by Jacob. The clay stove inside the home had an extended ledge used to dry wet clothing and moccasins. Sometimes, the children would lie or sit on the ledge to warm their bodies. Mary made mattresses for the beds from the hemp fibers grown and spun by the family. She filled them with hay. Mary also wove homespun hemp fibers into clothing for the family. She bleached sugar and flour sacks, using them to sew sheets, pillowcases, curtains, towels, children's clothing, plus cross-stitch embroidered scarves. These scarves were draped over religious pictures of saints, decorating the walls.

Coal oil lamps were the only form of lighting after dark. They had two lamps but Mary encouraged the family to use only one whenever possible to save on the cost. In the evening the older children and Mary all sat around the wooden table in the family room, working on their projects until bedtime. Mary always had many projects to work on, including sewing, mending, knitting, crocheting, embroidering, cross-stitching. The children loved to test each other on arithmetic and spelling questions. Jacob quite often worked at preparing strips of wood for building shelves, etc., while Mary and the children were busy after supper.

The family room in the home provided facilities mainly for cooking, eating, washing, and sleeping. In the early spring, cabbage and tomato seeds were planted in pots of earth and kept in this room in a sunny area. The seeds and plants required regular watering. Three to four dozen baby chicks also shared space in a corralled area. They had a much better opportunity to survive and grow in the warm environment. The chicks were very necessary in providing food for the family. The laying hens provided eggs. Hens that did not produce eggs, and roosters not required for the hens, were butchered for meat. The fresh meat and eggs were sold at the market; the produce not sold was utilized in the home for food.

A washstand for washing hands and face was placed outside, near the entrance of the home, and was used there as long as the weather permitted. It was then moved into the family room. Baths were taken infrequently in a porcelain tub placed on the floor in the family room. It was a challenge trying to be at the front of the line for a bath as the same water was used for the whole family. In winter, water was obtained by melting tubs of snow on the stove. Entertaining friends and relatives was also accomplished in this room.

The second room was considered the main sleeping room accommodating the parents and three youngest children. Michael and John slept on the floor in the family room on a mattress filled with hay. The other family members enjoyed the comfort of the beds. The beds were made of wood frames, and mattresses filled with hay. Bed covers and pillows were made with goose down.

Shelves were built of wood and attached wherever there was space, in all areas of the home. These shelves were used to store clothing, kitchen utensils, etc. A cloth curtain made of bleached flour or sugar sacks was attached to cover the shelves. Mary embroidered flowers on the bottom of the window curtains to enhance the charm in the home.

The summer kitchen was used for preparing and preserving fruits and vegetables, storage, and additional sleeping accommodation. When relatives visited and stayed all night, they slept on a mattress on the floor in the main room. Michael and John slept on a mattress on the floor in the summer kitchen when it was not too cold. The boys enjoyed this arrangement as it gave them more privacy and they could talk late into the night without disturbing anyone. Large barrels of dill pickles and sauerkraut were prepared in the fall and stored in the summer kitchen. As the cucumbers and cabbage fermented, odors were released and contained in the small room. At first the boys found the odors rather strong and heavy when they slept there, but gradually they adapted to them. The odor remained on their bodies and in their clothing for a couple hours in the morning. Sometimes they felt uncomfortable going to school, conscious of the odor. They would run most of the way, hoping the wind would freshen their bodies and clothing. By the time they reached the school, their bodies and clothing did lose much of the fermenting odor.

A VACATED FAMILY HOME

SIX

The barn, attached to the house under one roof, provided some heat to the home, while the cows where inside. During the winter, this was very much appreciated. During the summer, the cows attracted flies, which were a problem in the home, particularly with no screens on the windows and doors. Each morning the cows were taken to a grazing area in the valley and returned to the barn at approximately six o'clock in the evening for milking and the night. Family members took turns with this chore. In the event a cow strayed from the herd while in the meadows, one person from the valley remained in charge of them for the day. Each family in the valley was responsible for appointing a person for this chore approximately one day every ten days, based on the number of families. Children were required to take a day off school to attend the cows if an adult was not available. Michael and John shared this responsibility quite frequently but were not happy missing school. Milk and cream was sold as a source of income for the family so it was important for the cows to graze well. During the winter, the cattle were fed in the barn. This was additional daily work for the boys.

A variety of fruit trees, plum, chokecherry, apple, pin cherry and cranberry were located in the valley meadows, available to all families in the area. When Michael and John attended the cows together during the summer months, they also picked fruit. Their preference was picking plums and apples, filling their containers quickly. The boys also picked the other fruits required to make jam for the family. But they did not like being distracted from their main responsibility too long as some cows and calves could stray from the herd very quickly. Michael and John also picked fruit on days they were not attending the cows during the summer months. The early morning was a favorite time for them, using the remaining of the day to clean and prepare the fruit for preserving the next morning before the heat reached its peak, or selling the fruit at the market. John usually carried the picked fruit to the house at noon and took some to the market in the afternoon. Jean helped her mother prepare the remainder of the fruit for preserving in sealers.

Mary planted a variety of vegetables in the garden in the spring. She had approximately one-half acre of land at one side of the house cultivated by a neighbor. She then planted rows of many different seeds. Tomato and cabbage seeds were planted in boxes of soil, early in the spring, and kept in a warm place inside the home until the weather was appropriate for transplanting in the garden.

John did most of the weeding of the vegetable garden. He weeded some vegetables by pulling the weeds out by hand and used a hoe for others. Protecting the garden from the cows that were moved to and from the valley for grazing was sometimes difficult but very necessary as the vegetables were a main source of food for the family, plus a small income used for rent payment.

As vegetables ripened they were taken to the market for sale. The family utilized the unsold products in their daily diets, enjoying whatever was available. There was no waste. In the autumn, turnips, potatoes, carrots, parsnips and beets were stored in the cellar, a dugout in the ground under one area of the house. These vegetables were the main source of food during the winter months. John was able to manage the garden and do marketing during the summer. During the fall, when John returned to school, Mary took over this responsibility. She dressed the two youngest children in warm clothing and took them with her to the garden.

Paul loved to romp around and entertain Ann in the carriage while his mother was busy digging up the vegetable garden. Sometimes he would pull a couple of carrots out of the ground to eat. Paul used his mother's long skirt to wipe the dirt off his carrots before offering one to his sister. Ann loved to play with her carrot, periodically biting the small end of it. Paul quickly devoured his carrot and went back for more. Paul also liked to leave a bunch of carrots for a little rabbit that he saw close to the garden. Mary suggested that if the rabbit was fed, perhaps it would not chew at the vegetables in the garden.

SEVEN

The peasants in Ukraine, under Austrian rule, remained economically dependent on the landowners. The men left their families during the fall and winter to find work which was necessary to meet financial needs. They accepted any type of work that was available, and were paid very little for long hours of hard labor. Jacob usually left early in the fall and was gone until early spring. He did not see his family during this time except for two weeks during the Christmas holiday season.

It was practically impossible for a peasant to own land in Ukraine. Jacob had built dwellings on the land he was renting. He had made a verbal agreement with his landowner to put up the dwellings. He could purchase the small piece of land they were now renting, in five years' time, at a reduced market price. At the end of the fifth year, Jacob approached his landowner with a small sum of money as a down payment for this property. The landowner would only honor the agreement in exchange for cash, which Jacob did not have and could not raise or borrow.

Jacob was devastated and depressed. He had no one to turn to for assistance. His friends and relatives did not have money to loan him. The family had worked long hours, gradually building a small nest egg. Their goal was to purchase the property with a small down payment, then continue with annual payments until the debt was paid. The time and money spent in putting up the dwellings would not benefit the family as planned. It was a loss and Jacob was having difficulty accepting it. He was also having difficulty accepting the human side of this landowner and resented having to make rent payments to him. He hated the landowner with a passion and would do anything to avoid coming in contact with him.

EIGHT

M ichael's regular seat at the supper table was next to his father's right side, and Paul's was on his father's left side. John sat directly across from Michael. Jean sat next to John and his mother sat at the far end of the table close to the stove, across from his father. Paul was seated to the right of his mother. At suppertime, Jacob regularly initiated discussion with his two eldest sons regarding the events which had taken place that day. The boys enjoyed explaining to their papa in detail the progress in their activities. In their opinion, it was man-to-man talk and they were part of the team of providers for this family. The other family members listened to the conversation as they ate their meal.

"John, how many vegetables did you take to the market today?" Jacob asked.

"I had a wheelbarrow full of lettuce and radishes. Everything sold in two hours."

Jacob smiled. "Good boy, did you get the same amount of money as last time?"

"Yes. Mama has all of the money."

"Michael, how is the mother cow and new calf doing? Is the calf feeding well?"

"Papa, we do not have a problem with the new calf," Michael quickly responded. "We do have another big problem to talk about."

"What is it, son? Are you having trouble at school with the teacher? Or is it the girls?"

Michael blushed when his father mentioned the girls but did not reveal his secret. He was not going to mention his infatuation with the girl he had not yet met, and much younger than himself.

"No, Papa, it is not only I who has this problem. It is all of us, our family. I heard you telling Mama last night you are planning to leave for Canada soon, is that true?"

Jacob was taken by surprise with Michael's direct question. He was planning to wait until the immigration papers were finalized before informing the children of their relocation, now he had no alternative but to present the plan to them at the supper table. Jacob looked over to his wife, hoping she would assist and support him in this communication, but she remained silent, occupying herself with the baby in the cradle close by and keeping her head down. Jacob was aware his wife had become emotionally upset during each of their discussions regarding leaving Ukraine. He understood her concern in leaving her parents but hoped in time she would adapt to the concept and accept the move as a new adventure. Jacob had lost his parents in a drowning accident when he was eighteen years of age. He had one sibling, a sister, living in the next village. They did not have a close relationship, talked to each other at social functions but did not visit. Mary, on the other hand, was the only child and her parents lived close by and visited regularly. Jacob knew it was going to be extremely difficult for Mary to leave her parents. Deep down, he felt more comfortable traveling to Canada before Mary, not having to witness the sadness when she and her parents were parting. Jacob also realized there was a possibility Mary may decide to stay with her parents and not follow him to Canada. He would have to gamble on that possibility. Owning land in Canada was extremely important to Jacob and he would continue with their travel and relocation plans.

Jacob finished eating his last perogy, laid his knife and fork on his empty plate, pushed his bench back and inhaled deeply before beginning the explanation of the possible changes about to take place in their lives. The children were anxiously waiting to hear the plans for their family. "Children, I was waiting for some final news from immigration before letting you know your mama and I are planning on taking you to Canada. Canadian government agents have been to our village, speaking about homesteads available to new settlers. There is new land being opened up in Western Canada. I can buy 160 acres for ten dollars. It is our opportunity to obtain freedom from serving a landlord. We will own our land and the government will assist us in buying horses and machinery to get started in farming. I have enough money to buy the land and my passage on the ship. I will be leaving as soon as I receive my immigration approval, possibly in one month's time. You will leave later with your mother, when your immigration approval has been received and the vegetables have been sold at the market. The cows were sold last week but will remain here until you are ready to leave."

Jacob explained the position he was in with the present landowner; especially his being unable to purchase the property they called home even though he owned the dwellings. The landowner owned the forests and pasture, charging Jacob for cutting trees for fuel, and for pasturing the cows. Jacob stated he knew a man in the next village interested in purchasing the dwellings and its contents, and would pursue this sale. They would not be moved off the property until after Mary and the children had vacated them. The money received would be used to pay the passage costs for family members to Canada. They were going to the big country and Jacob would be purchasing a very large piece of land where they would be living. First, he had to go and build their home. The timber on the land would be used to build their home and maybe he could market some timber as well. Later, he would clear some land for gardening and agricultural purposes. Jacob expressed his desire for democracy and independence, plus a more comfortable lifestyle for his family.

Michael looked at John and Jean. They were staring at their papa, unable to speak. Paul wanted to know if they would be traveling in the wagon. Michael suddenly realized the thoughts penetrating his mind all day were now a reality. He also realized his mama was not happy with this move to a new country. He could feel the sadness she was displaying, saw her wipe the tears from her eyes. Quickly, he turned to John and Jean with a big smile.

"Papa is going to build us another house in Canada where we will have our own land and become big landowners. We will learn to speak another language and make new friends."

John and Jean listened to Michael with their eyes wide open. After a few minutes, they displayed some excitement, responding positively. Paul, of course, was most interested in how they were going to travel. Mary became a little more positive, delivering a partial smile to her family, when she realized the children were excited and anxious to know more details. However, she had many thoughts and concerns regarding this adventure, including not understanding the English language, leaving her parents and possibly not seeing them again.

NINE

At the turn of the nineteenth century, the liberal government in Canada actively promoted immigration from Ukraine. It was believed at the time that only farmers were desirable immigrants. If Britain, Northern Europe and the United States could not provide the required numbers of desirable immigrants, new sources of agricultural immigrants would be sought. The rural population of Southern and mostly Eastern Europe were the alternatives. Agents from Hamburg had traveled throughout Eastern Europe offering five dollars for every male immigrant and two dollars for each woman and child.

Offers to purchase a homestead property consisting of 160 acres for ten dollars attracted many impoverished peasants from Galicia to immigrate to Western Canada. Candidates who had adequate means and temperament for pioneering were selected and billeted in block settlements for psychological and practical reasons.

The qualifications possessed by most Ukrainian immigrants from Galicia: young, had some rudimentary education, some political experience in the constitutional system of Austro-Hungary, and spoke, or at least understood, Polish and German.

In a span of 30 years, approximately 600,000 Ukrainians left the Austro-Hungarian empire for North and South America. Several thousands also emigrated from the western regions of Russian-controlled Ukraine. Approximately 400,000, mainly laborers, landed in the United States; up to 150,000, predominantly agriculturalists, settled in Canada; some 50,000 headed for Brazil and Argentina.

The Canadian government promoted a campaign to open land in the "prairie provinces." The Canadian Pacific Railway demanded settlement of the country before building a railroad across Canada. Immigrants, mostly from Southeastern Europe, were sought. Canadian government agents visited the villages in Ukraine, presenting Western Canada in a very positive format with the promise of government assistance to begin farming. These agents received bonuses for their accomplishments in this very large immigration program: They sold ten-dollar ocean voyage tickets plus a promise of the purchase of a homestead for ten dollars. The picture of the farming process on the prairie provinces of Canada, as presented by its government agents to the peasants, was not accurate. Most settlers were severely deflated on their arrival, realizing how easily they had fallen for false promises.

The Ukrainians were latecomers in obtaining prairie homesteads in Canada; much of the best land was already taken. They settled on wooded land in close-knit communities to give each other support and assistance. Attempts were made to recreate villages similar to those they had left in Galicia or Bukovyna, hopefully masking the loneliness of the settlers and hopefully helping them adapt in their new country. Settlers chopped down trees with the axes they brought with them, pulled out tree stumps with their hands, dug up the soil with the hoes they had also brought with them. In the beginning, many settlers did not have horses or oxen. Women or men were harnessed to pull wooden plows. To earn money, the men walked many miles seeking work. They walked back home, carrying bags of flour on their backs from the closest village store.

The heads of families were often away from home for months at a time working as loggers, or farm laborers, or on one of the railways being built throughout Western Canada. The women experienced a hard and lonely life, caring for the family, responsible for all the chores, garden, etc. Many families did not have transportation; women walked many miles to the village or grocery store, hoping their credit would be accepted until some money was received from their husbands.

Few of the Ukrainians had much capital to equip a prairie farm. Government subsidies were not available to the Ukrainian settlers as there had been to the Mennonites and Icelanders who had arrived earlier. British neighbors resented the Slavic influx, and therefore provided little support. The distinctiveness of the Ukrainians—in dress, culinary habits, and especially in language and religion— was both a threat and a challenge to society.

Approximately two-thirds of the immigrants were Uniate Catholics, the remainder of them were Orthodox. Their clergy did not accompany them to Canada so they were vulnerable to the Roman Catholic Church, the Presbyterians and Methodists who wanted to increase their numbers. Most Ukrainians maintained their religion. They gained a sense of security when the first Catholic bishop arrived from Ukraine and Russian Orthodox priests served the Orthodox group from the United States, subsidized by the Russian church.

Retention of the Ukrainian language was considered crucial for community integration. It was a bond between the adult generation who had difficulty learning English, and the children who were quickly influenced by the English culture around them, especially when absorbed in the education system. Ukrainian was spoken in the homes of all the Ukrainian families, their churches, and community events. When children tried to speak to their parents in the English language, many parents insisted only Ukrainian be spoken. Unfortunately, these parents continued living in Canada without learning the English language. They depended on their children to translate for them. A newspaper, *The Ukrainian Voice*, published in Ukrainian, was enjoyed by many of the adult settlers.

Bilingual education in English and German, Polish or Ukrainian, was initially provided in the schools, but after a few years it was discontinued in favor of only the English language.

SETTLERS FROM UKRAINE

SETTLERS FROM UKRAINE

SETTLERS FROM UKRAINE

TEN

Two weeks after Jacob informed his family of their immigration to Canada, he received notification that his papers were approved and he had passage booked on a steamship leaving Hamburg, Germany, in ten days. On arrival at Hamburg he was to pick up his papers at the immigration center and a steamship passage from the booking agent. Passage and immigration for his wife and children would not be ready until the following year. Mary and the children had planned to leave later that year, so were rather shocked to hear of the delayed time for their departure. Jacob assured his family he would arrange for them to live in the house until their departure date. He would also delay the transfer of the cows to the new owners until their departure date. The family would continue having milk, cream, butter and cheese.

Jacob was excited about traveling to a new country and getting established on his own land. However, he became tearful when he thought about leaving his family behind. He was so positive about their future in Canada and was so anxious to begin preparing for his family's new home. These feelings gave him encouragement to move ahead.

Jacob decided he would need some tools to work his land. He was able to buy a large old trunk which he filled with some clothes, a pillow, two little pots, a few cutlery, a small feather bed cover, an axe, shovel, scythe, sickle and hoe. Taking these tools made Jacob feel self-sufficient, ready for his big challenge.

The ship Jacob sailed on was very old and in poor condition. This was a worry to him. Halfway across the ocean the ship lost power and started to take in water in the lower deck where the animals were located. The crew, with help from some of the young male passengers including Jacob, was able to bail the water out and prevent the ship from sinking. Many animals did drown. Two days went by before another ship came to their rescue, transporting the passengers to Montreal. Another ship would be arriving to transport the cattle and the crew to Montreal.

Jacob experienced a long and tedious voyage with feelings of anxiety regarding the possibility of the ship sinking. It was a relief to reach Montreal in Canada and then travel by train to Winnipeg, where he would be assigned his homestead which was situated close to relatives and friends he knew from Galicia. Jacob was very excited and felt ready to begin a new life in the very large acreage of trees, his new homeland.

Unfortunately Jacob did not have much time to clear the land before winter came. With the assistance of some cousins who had already settled in the area, he was able to build a small home using poplar logs. The area between the logs was plastered with a paste made of clay, mud, straw and water. The roof was covered with sod and hay. The stove and chimney were made of clay.

Jacob spent a portion of the winter cutting down trees for cordwood, which he sold. The remainder of the winter and spring were spent working at a sawmill. He was anxious to buy a team of horses and also enlarge his home to two rooms before Mary and the children arrived.

Jacob heard that a railroad was being built across Canada and got hired for this project in the local areas. He decided the money he earned would be helpful in getting started in farming. He also realized the need to meet government expectations in order to receive a deed for his land.

Mary and the children experienced a very cold winter with heavy snow, followed by heavy rains in the early spring. They were ready for travel when their immigration papers and steamship passages finally arrived the following summer.

ELEVEN

The steamship Mary and the children traveled on from Hamburg to Montreal did not provide cabins for them, as they were passengers traveling with economy tickets. The passage was rough. There were no conveniences. They all slept on the floor using their own bedding, in a room shared by many other passengers. Their wooden trunks were placed in a cubicle. The area next to the trunks was their home for the three-week voyage. Food was scarce and bathroom facilities very primitive.

Mary dried out several sacks full of bread made with eggs, and brought them with her. This was their main food. Sometimes, the attendants brought the children warm milk in which they dipped their dried bread. Occasionally, they received an apple each. The sea became rough at times, creating a wavy, rolling sensation, which affected Jean the most. She spent much of her time at sea sitting on a pillow in their cubicle with her arms draped over her stomach, not wanting to move around. She ate very little of the food available to them but kept sipping on cold tea. This sustained her until they reached Montreal.

On the last week of their voyage, Ann became ill with diarrhea. There was not a doctor or nurse on board and no medication to counteract the severe symptoms. Mary spoke with an attendant, requesting assistance in obtaining some fluids from the kitchen, including tea. The attendant understood Mary's request and was most helpful. She became very attached to little Ann and the family. Ann had become very lethargic, dehydrated, and was running a temperature. Mary became extremely exhausted caring for Ann. She kept offering Ann frequent sips of tea and water. Michael and John offered to take over from Mary and did so for short periods. Mary was concerned with the possibility of falling into a deep sleep and the children would not waken her if they were experiencing a problem. She wanted to make sure Ann received frequent nourishment even if she had to be woken up to drink the fluids. Mary thought the boys might have difficulty waking Ann, and not consider it a priority. After three days and three nights of apprehension, the diarrhea eased off and Ann began to show signs of improvement. She recuperated slowly, did not regain her strength for a few days, but was happy to rest and listen to the chatter of her siblings around her.

The last night on the ship was an anxious time for Mary and several of the children. Mary was anxious for their arrival in Montreal, for them to be off the ship. She was not able to sleep the first part of the night. After tossing and turning for approximately four hours, she drifted off into a deep sleep. Michael was excited about reaching land, woke up early, anxious to catch a glimpse of his new country. The sun was beginning to rise, illuminating a very beautiful picture on the water. Michael looked around to see if any family members were awake to share this beauty with him. Nobody was stirring. While glancing over the family sleep area, Michael was not able to focus on Ann. He took a closer look, thinking she may be under the covers. All of a sudden he heard a whimpering sound away from the sleep area. Was this sound coming from Ann? Michael got himself up in a flash and ran towards the area the whimpering was coming from. He jumped over passengers asleep on the floor. As Michael was running, he could see a small item on the floor at the far end of the passenger area, close to the railing. He recognized Ann's cry, knew he had to get to her before a strong wave came up. Ann's body was tiny and would not be protected by the railing because of the large spaces. Michael reached Ann, picked her up in his arms and held her close to his body. She was cold and wet. Mary was frantic when Michael approached the family sleep area with Ann in his arms. She had woken up when Michael was rushing away and did not realize Ann was missing. When Michael placed Ann in his mother's arms, Mary burst out sobbing. She was very disillusioned with herself, knowing what the consequences could have been.

The train ride from Montreal to Winnipeg, Manitoba, was long, but not nearly as long and uncomfortable as the steamship. The children were able to see the countryside and cities as they passed through. Mary was concerned about having enough food on the train, as she did not want to spend any of the money she had saved and brought with her. Fortunately, there was a family sitting close to her that became friendly and tried to converse with her. They did not speak Ukrainian but realized Mary and the children were new settlers, and needed food. The mother of this family spoke to the conductor about any left over food in the kitchen being shared with Mary and the children. Mary was elated when each day the conductor brought her several trays of foods she was not familiar with, but was quickly devoured by her and the children. Mary was beginning to feel good about Canada becoming her home. Michael and John became friends with two boys on the steamship and continued spending time together until the boys left the train in Winnipeg. The three other children were quite content staying near their mother.

TWELVE

Mary felt extremely tired from traveling and was looking forward to getting settled in her new home. Jacob had written two letters but did not offer much information as to his progress in building their home. The second letter indicated the house would be ready for them when they arrived. Mary's thoughts were constantly geared to their new life, wondering if they had made the right decision in relocating.

When the family arrived at their destination in northern Manitoba, approximately fifty miles from Dauphin, Jacob was there to greet them with a team of horses and wagon. Everyone was talking at once, asking Jacob many questions. After hugging and kissing them all, Jacob helped Paul and the ladies into the wagon. He asked the two eldest boys to help him load the trunks and then began the drive home. It was a special time that each family member would relate to and remember as the big change in their lives. Jacob had initiated this change and appeared to be happy, adapting well.

During the drive to their new home, Jacob talked about the work he was doing for the Canadian Railway, laying railroad tracks. It was only temporary work and very hard work, but he was happy to be able to work close to home. He felt good about helping to build Canada plus he was earning some money to help build their barn and develop their land. However, he was not able to spend time working on the barn and land when working on the railroad. This was a concern to him

After traveling approximately four miles in dense forest and rough road, the last two miles of road gradually narrowed into a trail. Mary was beginning to feel concerned about the uninhabited territory they were driving in and was wondering if their home was located in this area. She heard Jacob speak out loudly as he pointed to a building nestled in the woods, barely visible. "There is our new home and we are on our land, 160 acres covered with trees. I built the house close to the river. It curves through the corner of our property. I am also going to build a fence around the property to keep out the animals," he commented. Jacob was excited and anxious for a positive response from his family. Mary felt bewildered as it really was not what she was expecting, but she smiled at her husband and responded, "We will have a good life here, Jacob."

Michael and John jumped off the wagon before it came to a halt. They ran toward the river, talking about finding a swimming place. Jean, Paul and Ann appeared tired, expressing very little enthusiasm, wondering where they would sleep. They followed their mother into the house while Jacob attended to the horses.

The home was very small, resembling a thatched cottage. The front wall of the house contained the entrance door with a window on each side. There was no floor in the house and the only furniture was a long wooden table Jacob had built with seven stools, one for each family member, plus a clay stove, some wood for the stove, a few dishes and cutlery, a pail of drinking water with a dipper, used for drinking, and two pots for cooking.

Mary smiled as she entered her new home, examining the one large room and one much smaller room. It was primitive but something they could build on, she thought to herself. It felt warm and cozy. "Bring in the trunks," she informed Jacob as he entered the doorway. "We need to get settled. You look as though you have not been eating well, Jacob. Are you feeling okay?" "Yes, I am feeling really good but have missed your good cooking,

Mary. I am so happy you are here with me and we can begin our new life. I am sure I will soon gain back those pounds I lost."

After Jacob and the boys brought in the trunks, Mary grouped the children together and explained the layout of the home. The large room was their cooking and living area; the smaller room would be their sleeping area. "I will soon have enough lumber for the floor and will build a large clay oven outside for baking bread," Jacob announced. "That is good," responded Mary. "We will take our laundry to the river for washing now but when winter comes we will have to wash in the house. I will whitewash the walls inside to make the house brighter," she added.

"For sleeping tonight, we will have to bring in some dry grass to cover the damp floor," Mary continued. "Let's get started while the sun is still warm." Mary and the children tugged loads of dry grass to make a bed on the damp floor. In the morning they would have to carry it out to dry in the sun. Mary had some bedding in one of the trunks. She spread it around over the dry grass, suggesting the children share pillows and lay close together to keep warm.

When Jacob and Mary bedded down for the first night together in their home, they counted their blessings. They talked about their land, good black, rich soil, just like the land they left behind in Ukraine. "Only this land is ours," said Jacob, "and we have 160 acres of timber as well as soil, including jack pine, spruce, poplar, tamarack, elm, ash, and oak. I have picked mushrooms and many different berries; including saskatoons, blueberries, chokecherries, raspberries, strawberries, cranberries and also plums. We will be able to trap mink, weasel, muskrat, wolves, fox, black bear, and sell the furs. There is an Indian family living in their tent, in the woods, a couple miles from here. The man has offered to hunt with me. I think it would be good for me to get some trapping experience with him. We will have meat. I have seen deer, moose, partridges and rabbits. There will be fish in our river in the spring. We will enjoy catching them to eat immediately and dry some for the winter months. It is our homestead, Mary! Hallelujah!"

Unfortunately, the homestead land did not compare to the land Jacob and Mary left in Ukraine. This land was a mixture of sand and stones in some areas, black soil in small areas, swamp and marsh in large areas. The land was inhabited with many wild animals, deer, moose, elk, bear, wolves, fox, coyotes, along with many mosquitoes and flies in the summertime.

Clearing and developing the land was done by manual labor. Trees had to be chopped down with an axe and the branches all trimmed. The logs were cut up for cordwood and sold, cut up for firewood and used, or hauled to the sawmill and sold for lumber. A stump puller was man-made, providing a slow process in removing the stumps. Any remaining bush was burned. Money had to be earned to buy a plough and oxen or horses to break the soil for cultivation. Fortunately, Jacob was able to buy a team of horses with money he earned working on the Canadian Railway, but he did not have time to break up as much land as anticipated. The soil was cultivated using man-made equipment, discs and cultivators. Planting was done by hand, carrying a sack of grain on the back, scattering the seeds by hand. The grain was cut by hand with a sickle or scythe. There were no threshing machines. After the stocks of grain were tied into bundles and flailed, the chaff had to be separated from the grain. A blanket was placed on the ground. A small amount of grain at a time was shaken from a high level over the blanket, allowing the wind to blow the chaff away and the kernels of grain fall on the blanket. The grain was put through a wire sieve, removing the rough kernels. A hand-turned millstone, available in very few areas, was used for milling the grain into flour.

During the early years there were no grain elevators and farmers weighed their grain on platform scales before loading it into a boxcar. They received their money after the grain was sold. Harvesting became a challenge when eventually one threshing machine was available in the area. It was a waiting game. Neighbors had disagreements as to who was next in line for their grain stacks to be threshed. Some grain did not get threshed until late in the season, reducing its quality.

There were very few doctors in Northern Manitoba, and mustard plasters and patent medicines were used frequently in the homes. Garlic and onions were a popular food in health promotion. Wearing camphor bags as necklaces were used for colds and chest problems. Storekeepers traded cordwood for supplies that were needed by the farmers. Pork, butter, eggs, fish, furs and berries were also traded for groceries.

The farmers living in each district had the responsibility of building a school, if they wanted their children to receive an education. A farmer usually donated the land for this project. The farmers voluntarily cut down trees, sawed the lumber, and built a one-room schoolhouse and two-room teacherage. It took approximately two to three years before completion. The teacherage was a small home for the teacher to live in, as the families did not have room for a boarder in their home.

THIRTEEN

The Ukrainian newcomers received a free homestead, registered in the name of the family head. In return, each farmer had a goal to reach. They were expected to build a barn and home, prepare thirty acres of land for cultivation, buy a few farm animals, develop the land to produce food, and be self-sustaining, all within three to five years from the time their homestead was given to them. Settlers with more dense forest on their land were given up to five years. A government inspector would visit and approve their progress before a deed was issued. If approval was granted, the farmer was asked to pay the inspector ten dollars for a deed to the land. Jacob was anxious to meet this requirement and obtain a deed. He expressed this strong desire to Mary, hoping she would have the same enthusiasm. Mary responded positively, making Jacob feel good.

Each newcomer requested a homestead as near as possible to family members or friends. They could then work together and socialize in their own language, reducing times of loneliness in a strange country. Their preference was to have as much wood on their land as possible. The reason being, in Ukraine they had to pay, or work hard for the landlord in lieu of pay, for the privilege of obtaining some wood. Now they would always have wood available to them.

Mary had saved approximately twenty-five dollars and brought the money with her. She suggested to Jacob that they purchase a milking cow with a portion of this money. She was thrilled to be able to offer this assistance and Jacob was elated. The day after the family arrived, Jacob asked Michael to assist him in this purchase. They would have to travel with the horses and wagon to a prosperous settler's place and choose an appropriate cow. The cow would follow them home, tied to the back of the wagon.

The cow became a true friend of the family. She used to go into the woods to graze, but came home on her own when it was milking time. This was most fortunate as it would have been very difficult to find her in the dense woods, even though she carried a bell around her neck.

The roads for miles around were only trails. When visiting neighboring relatives, Jacob taught the family to mark the trails with sticks and cut notches on trees in order not to lose their way when returning home. Families in the neighborhood became very friendly towards each other. They assisted one another in every way, enduring the hardships of pioneering and overcoming homesickness. It wasn't long before Mary and Jacob had many friends as well as relatives in the area.

Jacob had prepared a small area of land and planted a garden before the family arrived. They had vegetables ready for use. With some of the money earned from the Canadian Railway, Jacob had bought one hundred pounds of flour and one hundred pounds of sugar for Mary to use in her cooking. He was happy to know his family would have food, including fresh bread. He was also looking forward to some "perogies" and "borscht", two of his favorite dishes. Mary brought some hemp, poppy and sunflower seeds with her and was anxious to plant them in the garden.

During the winter months, John learned to catch rabbits with a trap he made from twigs. He also learned to skin and clean them. This provided meat for the family. Jacob made socks and moccasins from the skins for the children.

Many skills were developed and used by the Ukrainian families as they learned from each other. Initially, wrinkled Sunday dress clothes were dampened and rolled tightly around a homemade rolling pin until dry. Later, an iron was available on the market. It was made of steel, in the shape of the present iron, only smaller and much heavier. A wooden handle was attached to the iron, controlling the iron on the clothing with your hand on the wooden handle. The iron was heated on the wood stove, requiring frequent re-heating. There was no temperature control. The iron had to be cleaned off before use, protecting the clothes being ironed from the smoke and dirt on the stove. Women not only managed the essentials in caring for their home, garden and family; they assisted in the fields, learned as many crafts as available, including spinning yarn, weaving, quilting, and feather stripping. They struggled in understanding the responses to the diseases experienced by them. Cleanliness became a priority. Men worked together clearing land, followed by cultivation, sharing traditional tools, expanding their houses, building barns for the animals, and granaries for the storage of grain. The work was never ending and very little land was cleared because of the extreme difficulty in the process. The tools they had were very primitive. There was very little economic gain; it was a bare existence, which became more frustrating each year.

UKRAINIAN DOLL
By—ZENIA

FOURTEEN

E ducation for the children began when the pioneers completed the building of a school. The plan was to hire a teacher that spoke both English and Ukrainian. However, that was not possible. An English-speaking teacher was hired instead.

The teacher, Mr. Day, began his teachings by commands and signs, progressing rapidly. He had great respect for the settlers. In his opinion, these families had courage and foresight to migrate thousands of miles into an entirely strange country, without knowledge of the language and customs, or the means of sustaining life for long. They must have lived in severe political and economic conditions; otherwise they would not have come to seek freedom in the wilds.

One young girl expressed herself, "Here is free land, and if there is land and strong hands, then hope, too, exists that better times will come."

The children were very anxious to learn and continued speaking the English language at home. Jacob and Mary were happy with the progress the children were making at school, but wanted the Ukrainian language spoken at home, just as other parents requested. This was their heritage and they did not want it to change even though they were in Canada and their children were changing by adapting to Canadian customs and lifestyles. It was confusing to the children but they tried to respect their parents' wishes. Very few parents in this group learned the English language. They were adamant not to sacrifice their language, religion and tradition.

Walking to school in the winter months was dangerous. The snow was deep; sometimes reaching the waist of a child. Many children left home in the dark and came home in the dark. Some days they experienced bitterly cold temperatures of thirty to forty degrees below zero. In the spring there was no drainage provided. This placed the children in the position of walking in the water and having wet feet and footwear. All families were concerned about the bears and other animals. Fortunately, there was a lot of food available in the woods for the wild animals, which kept them away from the humans.

Townships gradually provided land for public schools where one-room schools appeared, followed over the next generation or two by newer elementary and secondary schools. The educational movement slowly expanded. Male pupils became lawyers, doctors, dentists, pharmacists, teachers, mechanics, engineers, editors, and politicians, leading men in their communities. Female pupils became teachers, nurses, and secretaries. Young men fought in World War II, becoming worthy citizens.

Young adults in the community presented Ukrainian concerts. They walked six to eight miles for practice, rehearse for a couple hours, and then walked home. Ukrainian dancing and singing were very much enjoyed by the presenters and audience. Christmas Eve was celebrated on the eve of January 6 by preparing and serving twelve different meatless foods, followed by the children hunting for peanuts in the hay on the floor. Christmas Day was celebrated on January 7 at church, followed by singing carols at many homes. Easter Sunday morning was also spent attending church. Each family prepared a basket of food and brought it to church with them to be blessed. After the church service, the families returned to their homes and had dinner over the blessed food. It was felt the blessed food would contribute to their good health each year. Families praised the Lord, thanked him for their life in Canada, their great country, a land of freedom. Folk dances and folk customs, egg painting, festivals, music, religion, libraries, concerts, handicrafts, and many more activities, were parts of the total education of the Ukrainian newcomers. All of these contributions by the Ukrainians gradually blended into the patterns of what is called the Canadian mosaic.

UKRAINIAN DANCER

FIFTEEN

Michael enjoyed school but was anxious to find work that would earn more money than he was presently earning cutting cordwood with his father a couple days a week. He completed the seventh grade and was now sixteen years of age. It was time for him to be independent, he thought to himself.

Michael loved nature and had learned from his father and Indian friend how to survive in the wilderness. He was as adept as any native Indian. Michael loved the solitude and peace he experienced as he explored the wilderness while hunting with a twenty-two calibre rifle. He was happy to be instrumental in providing meat for the family.

Michael grew into manhood as a tall, slim, handsome man. He presented a captivating smile when he spoke, expressing his opinions extremely well. He loved to be a part of a group or family, showing a great interest in his own development and future economic stability.

The next Sunday, as the family was having their noon meal, Michael approached the subject with his parents. "I would like to quit school and find work to help with the family expenses and maybe buy some land for myself. I have studied hard at school and feel my education at the seventh grade in the English language is all I will need to make a good living. I really want to own my own land, like you do, Papa. The sooner I get started earning and saving money, the sooner I will have the land. You remember how unhappy you were when you had a landlord. I do not ever want to be in that situation."

Jacob and Mary agreed with Michael, as they were anxious for the older children to leave the home and be independent. Jacob could not resist reminding his son, "The only wife for you is a Ukrainian girl. Do not get mixed up with any other culture, stick to your own."

Michael had no thoughts of marriage. There was so much to accomplish before thinking of a wife. He had not met anyone in the neighborhood that he would be interested in. "I'll make sure you have a chance to check my girl out before I marry her, Papa," he replied.

The following day, Michael packed his clothing and personal items in a large cotton bag and asked John to go with him by horseback to a logging camp where he could begin work. John would stay overnight and return with the horse the following day. An Englishman, who lived near a wide river not too far from a town, owned this logging camp. Michael had information on how to get there and knew a couple men working there. He was excited about his transition into manhood and felt really comfortable in this challenge.

John felt sad about Michael leaving home as they had a good relationship and worked together on many projects. However, his thoughts kept returning on how he would now be the eldest of the children living at home and would be given more responsibility. When his father was away, he would be in charge of the horses, cutting firewood, and helping his mother when required. It made John feel very manly, a good promotion in his life.

John was considered to be a little short and stocky compared to Michael, and a little overweight. He loved his mother's perogies, fruit pies, fresh bread and cinnamon buns. John had a very soft voice and spoke in a low tone to his parents and siblings. They all loved him and found him very helpful in discussing family situations. Mary depended on him for many activities. Now that Michael was leaving home, Mary would be giving

John more responsibilities. John knew this and was looking forward to the challenges. It made him feel good to be an important part of the family. John loved his mother dearly and would assist her as much as possible.

SIXTEEN

Michael worked hard in the bush cutting down trees, skidding logs and hauling them to the sawmill. Some days he was asked to work at the sawmill, putting in long hours. The men lived in camp with primitive facilities, but the meals were good with large quantities of food available. They socialized in the evenings, mainly by conversing and playing cards. During Christmas and Easter holidays, they hitchhiked home to their families, celebrating the festivities with them. Michael loved going home loaded down with gifts for each family member. He purchased these gifts in the town near the sawmill. He could hardly wait to see the expressions on their faces as each family member received their gift.

After a couple years of working at logging and the sawmill, Michael decided to venture into a new life. During the voyage to Canada, he had talked to a couple young men who had relatives working on a large ship on the Great Lakes. This type of work appealed to Michael a great deal and he thought about the possibility of this venture. A co-worker at the sawmill had a friend who was a contact person in Fort William, and arranged for Michael to get in touch with him. During his Easter visit at home, Michael informed his family he would be heading out to Fort William to work on the ships.

Michael was excited about his plans, but also realized he did not have a definite job. He would ride the rails to Fort William to save money but he chose not to tell his parents of this mode of travel, as they would be worried. Fort William is located in the northern part of the province of Ontario, approximately six hundred miles from Michael's home.

On arrival at Fort William, Michael sought out Jack Dempsey, his contact person. Jack was most instrumental in directing Michael to the appropriate personnel. Jack also invited Michael to stay with his family until he had a job. After three days of interviews and paperwork, Michael was heading out to his first job experience on a ship, moving grain across the Great Lakes, then returning to Fort William for another load. He would not see land for months at a time. Michael could hardly wait to begin his first voyage. He kept thinking about his previous voyage across the ocean to Montreal from Ukraine.

Michael's job as a fireman (4th engineer) was to fire and feed the furnaces with coal to make steam. It was an extremely hot area and a number of the men collapsed from the heat. A co-worker sprayed cold water from a large hose on the men that collapsed, to revive them. Fortunately, Michael was not affected and was able to avoid the cold-water sprays to his body.

Michael was thrilled with his new work, eager to learn as much as possible from other crewmembers. He felt proud to be associated with the large vessel on an important mission, fighting the rough waters to reach their destination. For eight months Michael worked on the same ship with little time off. He didn't mind, as he missed his family and felt better keeping busy. The work was exciting to him and he felt good about his adjustment to the ship. It was also interesting to be visiting Montreal, his port of entry to Canada a few years ago. Michael felt so much more comfortable now, compared to how he felt on his arrival to Canada.

At the end of the shipping season, Michael had saved a little money and was looking forward to going home. He would have had a larger sum of money, had it not been for losses to card gambling, which reduced his funds. Gambling was also a new experience that he quite enjoyed. Michael did have one sad thought about going home, his brother John would not be there. John had followed Michael's footsteps and left school to work at the logging camp. Michael missed John and was hoping to spend some time with him even if he had to go to the sawmill to visit him.

Michael thought seriously about returning to the ship for a second season. He had said goodbye to his shipmates, indicating they would be seeing him soon.

SEVENTEEN

Helena, a clever, dynamic, young lady with very good looks and a slim, well preserved body, was identified by her brothers as the "catalogue girl." She loved browsing through the Eaton's and Simpson's catalogues, admiring the clothing she would like to make for herself. Helena was the eldest daughter in her family of eight siblings. She had four brothers and three sisters. She loved school and wanted so much to keep learning but at the age of thirteen, realized it was necessary to get work outside the home and assist the family financially. Her brothers were out working at the age of eleven and twelve. Helena helped her mother with the younger children while going to school but felt her sister could take over this chore. Helena's father had heard about a doctor's wife in Pine Falls needing help to care for her home and four children. He suggested to Helena that the grocery truck that stopped in the village would be going to Pine Falls and she could possibly get a ride with this truck driver. She should be prepared to stay and work when she arrived there. He would speak to the driver and maybe she could go next week.

Helena was immediately accepted for the position. She adapted quickly to the children and was readily accepted by Dr. and Mrs. Clark. Helena worked long hours, applying the skills she had learned at home and feeling good about learning new skills from Mrs. Clark. The family loved her, depended on her and treated her as a family member.

Helena was happy in her new environment, learning housekeeping at a different level but missed her family very much. After one and one-half years, she decided to leave her work at the Clarks and go home. Helena had been dating a very good-looking high school student, Jim Hearn, but did not feel comfortable in this relationship. She felt he was much more knowledgeable than she was and he was not Ukrainian. How would he fit into her life when not one family member had a high school education and her parents did not speak English? Jim sometimes made fun of Helena when she did not know the meaning of a word he used in their conversation. This made Helena feel unequal.

Helena sat by herself on the home-bound train, contemplating the next move in her personal life. Should she write to Jim as she had promised? Just as these thoughts were creating concerns in her mind, she looked up and saw a tall, handsome, mature gentleman walk by, looking at her and smiling with direct eye contact. He looked familiar. Who is this guy, she thought to herself. I could really go for him. Her heart seemed to be going faster and faster. After a few minutes she remembered him. He was a student at the school in Ukraine. She saw him one day but had not talked to him.

As Helena continued watching, Michael returned to his seat, walking very slowly with his shoulders held back and head held high. He felt her eyes on his body. This was a good time to make his move, he thought to himself. I will go and talk to this girl.

"Hello, I'm Michael Karpiak and I wondered if you would like to share a chocolate bar with me. What is your name?"

"My name is Helena Stasuk and I am traveling to my family in Duck River. I have been working for Dr. Clark and his wife in Pine Falls. Yes, I would really like some of your chocolate bar. Please sit down." Helena could not keep her eyes off Michael as he carefully sat down beside her.

"I am also going home to Duck River," Michael responded quickly. "You look familiar to me. Did I meet you at school?" he asked Helena as he sat a little closer to her, portraying the most radiant smile on his face, and sparkling brown eyes. Michael handed Helena a piece of his chocolate bar. Each of them devoured their share very quickly, appearing anxious to converse.

Helena smiled back rather shyly. "Yes, I think we went to the same school in the old country, Ukraine. I saw you there and you saw me but you didn't speak to me. You spoke to the older girls. They were your age. You look the same as you did then, only taller."

Michael quickly remembered the details of his first vision of Helena. She was even more beautiful now, developed into a voluptuous young lady. Being close to her sent his heart racing, along with a blushing feeling over his entire body. How happy he was that her family came to Canada and settled in the same area as his family.

Michael and Helena sat together the remainder of the train trip and conversed continuously, talking about their families, their present life and their life in Ukraine. They had an exciting few hours. Michael wanted to pursue this relationship further but was hesitant in moving too quickly.

When they reached their destination, Helena's brother Frank was there to meet her. Michael did not have anyone meeting him. His family was not aware of his homecoming. He accepted an invitation from Frank to stay at their home for the night. The next day Frank would assist Michael in getting home. Michael was very pleased with this arrangement, giving him more time with Helena. He would also have a chance to meet the rest of her family.

EIGHTEEN

Helena was extremely happy at home during the months following her return from Dr. and Mrs. Clark's residence. She loved being with her family and Michael visited on a regular basis. At first Michael stated he came to visit Helena's brothers, but gradually admitted to visiting her. Helena began looking through the Eaton's catalogue, studying wedding dresses and costs. With the money she had saved from working, she could purchase a beautiful wedding dress, Helena thought to herself, but Michael had not mentioned marriage to her.

Michael did not report to his ship in the spring. He kept busy cutting cordwood in the area. During the Easter festivities he and Helena discussed marriage and began planning their wedding. It was to be held at Helena's parents' home. Her brothers would build a wooden platform and all festivities would be held outside following the marriage ceremony at the Greek Catholic Church. Neighbors all around joined in to assist in the preparations and celebration. Home brew whiskey was to be made by Michael's father. Jacob fermented barley, potatoes and several other ingredients, achieved a distillation process by slowly boiling these ingredients. This substance, sometimes called "moon-shine", gave the drinkers a happy feeling and energy to dance and sing on into the night. Michael's mother was arranging to make hundreds of perogies and put aside a barrel of dill pickles. Helena's mother was arranging for hundreds of cabbage rolls plus roasting a dozen chickens. Other family members would bring bread and headcheese. Helena baked a large three-tier fruitcake and was having a friend decorate it as their wedding cake. There was so much excitement for many miles around.

Fortunately the day of the wedding was warm and sunny. Following the church service, food was arranged on a long table on the wooden platform at Helena's parents' home. Two brothers living in the neighborhood played the violin and the guitar, providing music for dancing. Polkas were the favorite dance for everyone, young and old alike. Everyone had a good time all afternoon and into the evening until dark. The next day, everyone returned to continue the festivities until all the food and home brew were "demolished." It was a memorable occasion for everyone.

The bride and groom were exhausted following the festivities. The polka was played frequently and everyone wanted a dance with the bride or groom. The "Kolomayka" was also a big enjoyment with the younger crowd, a very active dance, requiring a great deal of energy. Helena's mother suggested Michael and Helena remain with her family for a few days and get some rest. Helena's brothers were excited about having the bride and groom stay with them. They quickly offered to prepare a special sleeping area for them. It was located in the hayloft in the barn. The bed for the bride and groom was made with layers of hay, covered with a quilt to sleep on. A small blanket was placed at the foot of the bed for a cover up, if required during the night. One feather pillow was to be shared. Michael and Helena were delighted with this special attention and privacy.

When Michael and Helena went into their sleeping area to bed down and make love for the first time, the only other activity in the barn was the cows below them, chewing, and periodically moving around in their stalls where they were located for the night, and for milking in the morning. A small lantern hanging on a wall, close to their bed, was their only lighting. It was very dim. Michael and Helena became a little nervous when they realized they were finally alone. It was their time together. "What a beautiful setting," Michael whispered to Helena as he reached for her and held her close in his arms, enjoying the immediate warm response from her. Helena loved hugging and kissing with Michael, but was very shy in any advances he made. Michael gradually encouraged Helena to join him in becoming more intimate with him, exploring with each other. They were soon feeling an abundance of warmth and excitement. "How beautiful love is," thought Helena. The next thought that came to her was what did her mother tell her about getting pregnant, was it an unsafe time before or after her monthly period? While Helena was pondering this issue in her mind, she realized Michael had reached his desire. Her immediate concern was whether she would get pregnant the first time they made love.

Michael and Helena spent time together during the day walking in the woods, talking about their future, enjoying each other. When it was bedtime, the brothers and sisters all said goodnight and disappeared. Michael and Helena loved their private accommodation. It was a beautiful, memorable experience in their lives.

WOMANHOOD

A girl becomes a woman
When she feels warm to touch
Sharing joy and togetherness
With the one she loves so much
She radiates love around her
Expresses happiness in her eyes
Her life is filled with laughter
Even though she sometimes cries
  A woman loves, a woman cares
  A woman gives, a woman shares
A girl becomes a woman
When she approaches each day
With an air of confidence
Making time for work and play
She creates many pieces of beauty
Is resourceful, true and fine
Her body portrays womanhood
A picture of love, so divine
  A woman loves, a woman cares
  A woman gives, a woman shares

MANHOOD

A boy becomes a man when he feels the need to share
His time, plans and lifestyle with someone who will care
He initiates a warm climate, expresses feelings of the heart
Longs for more time together, is not happy being apart
He feels it is a gamble, prepares himself within
Is cautious in his progress, not certain of a loss or win
The relationship begins slowly, gradually opening a new door
A love growing endlessly, with so much more in store
A boy becomes a man when he adapts to the unplanned
Respects the needs of others, manages life in high demand
Realizes a close relationship has pluses and minuses, too
Problems are resolvable when there is faith in "I love you"

PART TWO

Michael and Helena

MICHAEL, HELENA, and CHILDREN

HELENA and CHILDREN

NINETEEN

M ichael and Helena began their married life living in very close proximity to Michael's family, using the summer kitchen as their residence. Jacob insulated the walls and ceiling, built some shelves, a bed frame, plus a table and two stools for them. A cook stove was given to them from Helena's family. Many of the wedding gifts were household articles, so they were in use immediately. Michael enjoyed coming home to a well-prepared meal, anxious to know the changes and additions Helena was making in providing a warm, homey atmosphere.

Michael returned to logging with his papa while Helena enthusiastically worked on mproving their small home. She had bought a second-hand Singer sewing machine while working at Dr. and Mrs. Clark's home. Helena was very quick at learning to sew. She accomplished many projects, making curtains, pillow covers, tea towels, etc., for their home, plus clothing for herself and Michael. A couple months following their wedding, Helena was not feeling well. She had not menstruated that month but thought her period was late in coming because of all the excitement and changes in her life. As time went by and she missed her second period, she realized the sick feeling she was having was related to pregnancy, not exhaustion.

Mary and Helena worked in the garden together, hoeing and weeding. They chatted as they worked and were comfortable together. Helena was anxious to learn any new gardening and homemaking skills from her mother-in-law.

During the time when Helena was not feeling well, she came to the garden a little later in the mornings. Mary assessed her daughter-in-law's situation and surmised she was pregnant. After a few days, she approached Helena. "Are you going to have a baby?" Helena blushed a little. "I think so." "Does Michael know?" "No, I wasn't sure so didn't tell him." Mary immediately discussed pregnancy with Helena and assured her, based on her assumptions, she was pregnant and should tell Michael.

Mary was elated about her coming grandchild but was a little concerned how Michael would accept the news. He had expressed the need to own land before having children, the need to be established. Mary also felt Helena was very young, needed assistance and support. She would help Helena as much as possible.

Michael was very conservative with his feelings when Helena reported the news of her pregnancy to him that evening. He did not react, remained deep in thought, as he looked straight at Helena. "Are you sure?" "Yes, I am sure. I talked to your mother and she agrees with me." "Well, I guess we're going to have a baby," Michael responded. He smiled as he continued, "It looks like our family will come before we are landowners." Helena felt a little sarcasm in his comment but did not accept the comment as Michael's true feelings. After all, she thought to herself, he is always very enthusiastic in making love, and does not want to consider avoiding sex during unsafe times. How can I stop from getting pregnant?

During the remainder of the pregnancy, Helena felt Michael had distanced himself from her, spending more time with his parents in the evenings. Helena kept herself busy knitting and sewing for the baby along with the housework. During the fall months, she worked with Mary, getting the vegetables in from the garden and preparing them for the winter storage. During the winter months, darkness and exhaustion came before supper and Helena was happy to get to bed early. She was concerned about the delivery of the baby but Michael and his mother assured her there was a lady not too far away that delivered many babies. Michael would go for this lady when it was time. Helena wondered how she would know when it was time and what would happen if Michael happened to be working a long way in the woods when it was time? These thoughts came to her frequently as she lay in bed before falling asleep. Helena wished her mother lived closer to her to give her some support. She could not depend on her mother coming to visit very often as she herself had a large, young family to care for, with very little assistance from Helena's father. Helena's mother would not be available to help her during and after the delivery. Helena felt alone but realized she should be grateful having Michael's mother nearby.

TWENTY

H elena was anxious for winter to pass and for the baby to arrive. However, deep down, she was frightened and lonely for her family. She did not reveal these feelings to anyone. There was so much to learn about this pregnancy, the birthing and being a mother. On some days she wondered if she was truly capable of handling these responsibilities. Helena was determined she would not fail and decided to move ahead.

Helena's father obtained work at a sawmill away from home. Her mother had a big responsibility caring for the younger family members and did not have transportation for visiting. One horse was left for the older boys to ride to the village to pick up the mail and buy the staples, sugar and flour.

Michael's mother did not recommend traveling on rough roads during the last few months of pregnancy. Helena and Michael followed Mary's advice and suggestions pertaining to family care and lifestyle so the couple did not visit Helena's family. That left Helena on her own, at home most of the time. It was a very long winter for her.

As March came around, the few days of warmer temperatures which were experienced were not enough to melt the snow. Michael was hoping the baby would arrive soon as it was easier traveling by sled on the snow than by wagon in the mud. Although Michael had a fast team of horses that functioned best on the snow, the trip to the midwife's home would take a while, it being about five miles away.

March winds brought more snow with temperatures remaining cool until the last week of the month. The days then became warmer with snow becoming soft and melting. After enjoying the warm sunshine for a couple days, Helena was awakened early one morning with labor pains. She quickly woke Michael with the news. "The pains are starting. I think the baby will be coming. Please go for the midwife!"

Michael jumped out of bed, dressed quickly and left the house. After a few minutes he returned with his mother. "Mama will stay with you while I'm gone, Helena. She will take care of you."

Shortly after Michael left for the midwife, his brother Paul and sister Ann came running in to see what was going on. They heard the activity and wanted to know if their niece or nephew had arrived.

"The baby will not be coming for a while," explained Mary. "You can get ready for school. I don't think the baby will be born until this afternoon. You will probably be able to hold and admire your niece or nephew when you come home from school."

"Yes!" added Helena. "You will be able to help me care for the baby after a few weeks, when he/she gets a little bigger. Right now I need to be alone with your mother until the midwife comes. The pains are coming more frequently. Please leave us alone."

TWENTY-ONE

When Michael started on his journey for the midwife, Mrs. Nash, he was able to travel at a fairly good pace. The horses were fresh after a good night's rest and the temperature remained cool, preserving the snow on the narrow, unutilized road. However, as morning passed and moved into the noon hour, the sun became stronger and warmer. Michael could feel the slush on the roads. The horses were losing footage and had reduced their speed to a slow pace. Michael would have to feed and water the horses before returning. Fortunately, he would be at Mrs. Nash's home very soon and would attend to the horses while Mrs. Nash prepared to leave with him. Hopefully, she would not take long in her preparation, Michael thought to himself.

The road into the Nashes' home was treacherous with many ruts filled with water. As Michael raced into the yard, he could see a man and woman walking towards the house from the barn. Thank goodness she is here! he thought to himself.

When Mr. and Mrs. Nash saw the horses and Michael coming, they stopped and waited until he drove close to them. They had not met Michael and so did not recognize him.

"Hello! I am Michael Karpiak; my wife is having a baby. Mrs. Nash, can you come with me to help us deliver the baby? I will feed and water the horses, and then we can leave. We really need your help. My wife is frightened and I am too. My mother is with my wife and she has had children but does not feel competent in being responsible for my wife and the baby during the actual birth. She will be there to help you."

Mrs. Nash had learned midwifery from her mother who had been taught by their friend, Dr. Johnson. She was the only person in the area that could help in the delivery. Knowing this, Mrs. Nash immediately packed some clothes and utensils, a lunch for her and Michael to eat while traveling and was waiting for Michael when the horses had been fed. Mr. Nash did not appreciate his wife leaving for days at a time, but knew how much she was needed and how much she loved midwifery work. He said goodbye to his wife and Michael and went into the house to eat the lunch that his wife had prepared for him.

During the trip back, Michael was not always able to drive on the road as the snow had disappeared in some areas. He had to steer the horses to the side of the road, sometimes going over small, barren bushes. The trip home took longer and Michael showed anxiety as he responded to Mrs. Nash's questions about Helena's labor. "I only know she was having pains and I arranged for my mother to stay with her."

The sun was still shining when Michael and Mrs. Nash reached their destination. Mrs. Nash quickly stepped down from the sled and walked towards the house carrying her bag. She hoped the baby would be ready for delivery soon, before dark, as the coal oil lamps did not produce effective lighting for this procedure.

TWENTY-TWO

Helena was having frequent contractions, trying to get some relief from the pain by walking around the room. Mary was sitting by the window watching for Michael and Mrs. Nash. She kept talking to Helena, trying to calm her and assure her that the pain she was experiencing was normal. "You will forget about the pain after the baby is born," Mary commented. "No, I will always remember it," replied Helena, "It is continuous now. I wish Michael would hurry up."

Mary spotted the horses coming and breathed a sigh of relief. "I see them coming now! she quickly yelled out to Helena. I will go out and tell Mrs. Nash to hurry." Mary quickly went out the door and beckoned them with her hands to come quickly. "Quick! Quick! The baby is coming!" she hollered.

Mrs. Nash increased her walking speed to get to the house as quickly as possible. She slipped on some slush close to the entrance, but fortunately was able to control a possible fall by grabbing some twigs on a tree, keeping her body upright.

"I need some boiling water and lots of towels," she informed Mary as she put her arms around Helena, who was sitting on a stool at the table, crying with pain. Mrs. Nash noticed the wet floor under the stool and realized Helena's membranes had ruptured. She quickly escorted Helena to the bed and tried to take off her clothing but the labor pains were too severe. Helena managed to slip off her lower undergarments with the help of

Mrs. Nash. "It's coming! It's coming!" Helena shouted. "Yes, it is, Helena. Push down and help the baby." Helena gave a big push and the baby's head could be seen. She gave a few more big pushes and the head came out followed by the rest of the baby's body. It was a very fast delivery.

Mary had a large pot of water on the stove prior to Mrs. Nash's request and was happy to announce this as she handed Mrs. Nash the towels. She was at the bedside when the baby arrived. "It's a boy, Helena! It's a boy!" Mary announced.

As Michael walked in the door, he heard the news and was elated. He placed himself next to his mother at the bedside and smiled as he reached for Helena's hand. "You really did well; you brought us a boy, Helena."

Mrs. Nash placed the baby on a large towel after cutting the umbilical cord and carefully examined the baby's body. The strong cry indicated all was well. After wrapping the baby, she placed him in Michael's arms. "Why don't you put the baby in the cradle, and think of a name for your new son? Helena and I have some work to finish up and will need Mary's assistance. After I finish with Helena I will bathe the baby."

As Michael sat watching over his son in the cradle, he had difficulty realizing he was now a father. He quickly went back to his dream of being a landowner. It seemed so very far away now. "What are we going to call him, Michael?" he faintly heard Helena ask. "Why don't we name him after my father," Helena suggested. "No, we will call our son Bohdan, a strong name just like my strong grandfather I never met," replied Michael. "That is a good name for our son," Helena agreed.

TWENTY-THREE

T he summer passed quickly for Helena. She was busy with Bohdan, the garden, two cows to milk and feed, plus the housework. Even though she was alone many weeks at a time while Michael worked at the sawmill, she found comfort in having Bohdan. Each day brought so much joy to her as Bohdan cooed and smiled when she talked to him. Helena loved poetry and enjoyed reciting poems she learned at school to Bohdan. One of her favorites was:

> When you have work to do, boys
> Do it with a will
> Those who reach the top, boys
> First must climb the hill

Helena thought about trying to write poetry and did make an effort. Unfortunately, with her progressively busy schedule, she felt it was more important to use her energy on the needs of family and home.

Bohdan was very content playing outside in a seat made by his grandfather, and watching his mother as she spent many hours working in the garden. When Bohdan fell asleep, Helena would carry him to the house, place him in his bed and catch up on her housework until he woke up, then return to work in the garden with him.

When fall arrived, Helena experienced the feeling of pregnancy again. Her mother-in-law had informed her she would not get pregnant as long as she was breast-feeding. She had a couple of small menstrual periods and so thought the nausea may be caused by something else. Her breasts became sore but she thought it was from Bohdan's feedings. As the symptoms continued, she realized that pregnancy was a reality: She was going to have another baby.

Helena loved Bohdan and knew she would love her next child equally as much, but was hesitant in telling Michael about her situation. During his next short time at home, Helena casually mentioned it would be nice for Bohdan to have a sister or brother to play with. Michael became very angry and agitated. "There will be no more children in this family until we have our own land. The sawmill has slowed down so that means I will not have much work. There are so many men looking for a chance to work. I will have to stay and live at the camp, even though there will be many days of no work. Helena, I do not want to be pressured into more mouths to feed. It is enough for me having you and Bohdan."

Helena became very quiet, tending to Bohdan and preparing supper. What was she going to do? She decided to keep the pregnancy her secret as long as possible. Maybe when Michael came home for Christmas, he would be in a more jovial mood and accept the situation without revealing his deep feelings. After all, he was a participant and equally responsible for this pregnancy. The time that Michael spent at home was geared very much to sexuality. Helena did not always feel sexually inclined, but felt it was her duty to respond to her husband's desires and needs, particularly when he was away from home for weeks at a time. She never refused his sexual advances.

That evening, Mary came over to visit and play with Bohdan before he went to bed. She stayed for a while longer, chatting with Michael and Helena. She sensed the quietness in Helena. "Are you not feeling well, Helena? I noticed you were later coming in the mornings to shred cabbage this week. You wouldn't by any chance be expecting again?"

"No, I had work in the house to do first; Bohdan also had a runny nose so I waited until it warmed up a bit before taking him outside."

Helena's response appeared to satisfy Mary, and Michael did not present any questions. A few days after Michael left for the sawmill, Mary came over, carrying a casserole of cabbage rolls. "I thought you might enjoy these for supper, Helena. I'm concerned about you. Are you troubled about something?"

Helena had been extremely troubled and did not know how she was going to deal with the situation. When Mary showed compassion towards her, Helena burst out crying and blurted out her concerns. Mary put her arms around Helena. "It's not that big of a problem. You and Michael are young parents and can expect more children. That is normal. Do you want me to talk to Michael when he comes home?"

"No, no," Helena replied. "He will not be back until Christmas. By then my body will be changing and I will not have to say much. Thank you for coming. I feel better after talking to you. Thank you for the cabbage rolls. I feel hungry and will have them for supper. I hear Bohdan awake now."

Helena walked to the far corner of the room and picked up Bohdan from the cradle. His nose was runny and he had a cough. When Mary saw him, she realized he was not well. His face was flushed and warm to touch.

"Give him some water to lower his fever, Helena, and I will make him a mustard plaster later. Tonight we will make a tent with a sheet and make steam with kettles of hot water. I will be back after supper." Helena was so relieved to have Mary close by to help her with Bohdan. She was not comfortable caring for him when he was ill.

Helena heated up a few cabbage rolls for her supper but was not able to leave Bohdan long enough to eat them. He cried and coughed, his breathing becoming wheezy. She carried him around the house, holding him upright, patting his back, until he dozed off. Then she was hesitant in laying him down, in fear he would waken, so she sat on the side of the bed and rocked him back and forth until Mary returned.

When Mary arrived with a mustard plaster, kettle, and sheets, Bohdan woke up. Mary felt he was more lethargic than he was earlier but maybe it was because he had just woken up. She reached for him and offered to give him some water. Helena suggested she breast-feed first as he had not taken much milk earlier.

Helena waited until Bohdan became more awake before breast-feeding. He took a little feeding but not the usual amount. She spent more time coaxing him but was not successful. He became more irritable as she persisted with the feeding.

Mary prepared a bath for Bohdan while Helena was feeding him. "Let me take him for a while. I will bathe him and try to bring his fever down. Then maybe he will take some water. Helena, take some time out and have a little supper. You need to keep good nourishment in your body for yourself, for Bohdan, and for the new baby developing in your womb."

Helena was relieved to have Mary with her and expressed to Mary how much she appreciated her help with Bohdan. Mary indicated she had experienced the care of sick children and was happy to be able to help Helena care for Bohdan. Helena was not prepared for this crisis, having a sick baby with Michael away. She was hoping Mary would offer to spend the night with her. She was trying desperately to remember what her mother did when one of her brothers or sisters had a bad cold. Helena recalled how her mother stayed with the sick child and had her, the eldest child, care for the other children. Helena wished her mother lived close by to help her. If only she could talk to her!

Mary stayed with Helena until late that night, setting up the steam tent with sheets over Bohdan's cradle along with kettles of hot water under the sheets. The mustard plaster and steam were effective in loosening up Bohdan's cough. By morning his body felt cooler and he appeared less lethargic, more interested in feeding. When Helena talked to him, he responded with a smile. Helena was elated. When Mary arrived to check on Bohdan, she was thrilled. "It looks as though he is much better. We will watch him and maybe give him more steam tonight. I will be back later this afternoon."

"What about a doctor?" Helena asked. "Is there a doctor that would come out to help us with Bohdan? How can we get a doctor?"

The only doctor I know of is about 30 miles from here and someone would have to bring him here. It is a long way for the horses to travel and Bohdan is better now. "Helena, he will be fine." Helena thought about the doctor she used to work for. I wish I could talk to him, she thought to herself, but knew it was not possible. "I will keep praying and watching over my baby! I love him so much!"

TWENTY-FOUR

D uring the next few days, Bohdan's fever continued to remain lower, his body felt cooler, but his cough persisted. Mary assisted Helena each evening with a mustard plaster and steam. Helena was concerned that Bohdan was not feeding well and encouraged more frequent feeds. She was not getting much sleep. His breathing was very disturbing to her. It did not appear normal. Even when Bohdan did sleep for short periods, Helena watched over him, hoping to see some improvement in his condition.

Approximately one week after Bohdan first developed fever, Helena suggested to Mary that Michael be contacted to come home. If she could get Michael home, then maybe he would make some arrangements to get the doctor, she assured herself. Mary agreed that Bohdan's cough was lingering and he had not recovered as she had expected. She would ask Jacob to ride to the sawmill for Michael as soon as possible.

Helena felt relieved that she would have Michael at home soon to help her. When Bohdan woke up from his most recent short nap, Helena noticed his color was not as pink as it had been, he seemed a little gray and more lethargic. After a couple of hours, he seemed to pick up and his color seemed more normal. However, he was not feeding well and refused the water in the bottle. His diaper had very little urine.

The wood box was getting low and needed refilling, but

Helena hesitated in leaving Bohdan unattended to bring in the wood. When he coughed excessively, she would pick him up and pat his back. This seemed to help him. Mary was outside talking to Jacob before he left for the sawmill. Helena beckoned to Mary and asked her to come and stay with Bohdan while she filled the wood box and brought in a few pails of water. "Okay, Helena, I will come but first I must put some wood in my stove so the fire does not go out. It is getting close to winter and the house gets chilly without a fire."

When Mary approached Helena's house, Helena was all dressed, ready for her chores. Bohdan was asleep so Helena was anxious to get finished before he woke up. However, the noise of the wood as it went down into the wood box woke him. He woke up very irritable, crying, with a choking cough. Mary picked him up immediately and tried to console him. She realized then that Bohdan was much sicker now. He had lost weight and was pale. His breathing was raspy. He looked like her first baby did, just before she died. The death was caused by pneumonia, the doctor wrote on the death certificate. Was her grandchild going to die, too?

TWENTY-FIVE

Two days passed before Michael and Jacob returned. By then Bohdan had become very ill, clinging to life. Helena and Mary watched over him during the day and night, caring for him, but could not see any improvements. His condition was deteriorating, they were not able to help him, and they were getting very little rest.

When Michael walked in the house and looked over at Bohdan's cradle, he saw Helena and Mary, one on each side of the cradle. By the expressions on their faces, he knew things were not good. Helena's eyes were red from crying.

"Michael, thank God you are here. Can we somehow get a doctor? Our son is very ill. I think he is going to die!"

Michael put his arms around Helena as he looked down at their sick child. "The reason we were so long in coming, we did drive away out of our way to bring a doctor with us but unfortunately he was not there. He had just left his place to help a woman who was bleeding after delivering her baby. I arranged for the doctor's neighbor to bring him here as soon as he gets back home. I don't know of any other doctor for miles around."

Michael tried talking to Bohdan, caressing his face, but did not get any response. "He has been like this for the last few hours, Helena commented. I cannot wake him up. He sometimes does not breathe for a short time and I think to myself he is dead, and then he breathes again. I think he is going to die, Michael, if we can't get a doctor."

"I know Bohdan is very ill, Helena. Let's hope and pray for the doctor to come soon. Mama, is there anything we can do until the doctor comes?"

"We have tried everything that I know. At first Bohdan seemed to improve but then he got worse in his chest. The steam and mustard plaster didn't help him after awhile. I think we should keep turning him from side to side when he is in his cradle. Helena keeps trying to get him to breast-feed but he will not wake up. I think she should keep trying. Now that you are home, Michael, I'm going to catch up with my work and do some cooking. Your young sister, Ann, and brother, Paul, have been looking after the housework for me after school. Jean is helping a family with the children for a couple weeks while their mother recuperates from pneumonia. Jean attends school from their home. If you need me, just come over and get me anytime."

Mary had a strong feeling that Bohdan was not going to live. She should prepare some food for a possible funeral but did not want Michael and Helena to know what she was doing. They needed her support for their child's life, not his death. She would talk to Jacob about the situation and prepare him, as he would have to notify Helena's family. It was a fairly long journey.

When Mary returned to her own home, it was close to suppertime. As she opened the door, a wonderful aroma greeted her. Ann was busy at the stove, stirring something in a big pot.

"That sure does smell good, Ann. is it borscht? How did you get all the vegetables ready in such a short time?"

"I came home from school early today, Mama. The teacher knows Bohdan is very sick. She asked me this morning if the doctor came. I told her that my little nephew was not better, he was worse and papa had gone for Michael. There was no doctor yet. She told Paul and I to go home at noon, so we did. Paul cleaned the house, brought the wood and water in, and I made a big pot of borscht for us. Is there any thing else we can do to help?"

"That is wonderful, Ann and Paul. You are a wonderful family. I know your papa would appreciate some help with the barn work, Paul. When the borscht is ready, Ann, would you take some over to Michael and Helena?"

"I will, Mama. I want to see little Bohdan. I miss him so much when he is not able to come over to be with us. I don't want anything to happen to him."

"We are in the hands of God, Ann. I guess we will have to accept whatever he chooses for us. I know it is not easy, but that is how life flows, my dear. I thought I was going to lose you and your sister, Jean, on the boat when you were both so ill, but here you both are, beautiful strong, healthy girls. Maybe we will be lucky again."

TWENTY-SIX

E arly the next morning, little Bohdan took his last raspy breath. Michael and Helena were both beside him at the cradle. Helena had very little sleep the last few nights and was extremely exhausted. When the boy died, Helena could not control her emotions. She wept bitterly until her body became weary. She lay on the bed motionless and exhausted.

As Helena rested on the bed, she was reminded of the "life" inside her by the periodic kick-like movement she felt within. I have lost one baby, but I must not let anything happen to the one inside me, she thought to herself. I have not eaten or slept much but I'm not hungry. I know my baby needs food.

Helena kept trying to think which food she would possibly eat. As her thoughts kept focusing on this issue, she dozed off into sleep. Before noon she awoke to the voices of Michael and Mary. Immediately the death of her child returned to her mind. She quickly stood up and walked to the cradle where her husband and mother-in-law were standing.

Mary had dressed Bohdan in a little white gown that she had made for his christening, which was to take place just before Christmas.

"I hope you had a good rest, Helena. You needed it. I thought it would be appropriate to dress Bohdan in the christening dress I made for him. People will be coming to pay their respects later today and tomorrow before the funeral. Jacob has gone to notify your family and will bring a priest back with him. We can use our house for the wake as it is bigger and I have a couple ladies preparing the food."

"After the service tomorrow, Michael and Helena, we will have to bury Bohdan. Jacob and I found a beautiful big tree at the corner, near the river. Would you like to bury Bohdan under this tree? Jacob has made a wooden cross to place on the grave. Would you like to carve Bohdan's name on the cross, Michael?"

While Helena was standing, listening to Mary, Michael realized that Helena's abdomen was protruding. He had not noticed it during the night as Helena had a large, loose nightgown on when he arrived. Yesterday she had one of his shirts on, which was large for her. Mary noticed the observations Michael was making and decided it was a good time for her to leave.

"Helena, do you have another baby inside? You look bigger to me."

"Yes, Michael, we are going to have another baby. Maybe it is a good thing because God has taken Bohdan from us. I was waiting until you came home for Christmas to tell you, but now you know."

"Helena, I know I told you that I didn't want any more children until I was a landowner. Well, I'm thinking about buying a farm quite a ways south of here. An English farmer has a quarter section to sell and I have some money for a down payment. I need some more money to get started. I may ask your brother Jack, if he wants to go in partnership with me, then we will have money for machinery, animals and for getting started. Jack told me a few years ago he would like to farm but could not afford land that was already cleared. This land is half cleared and has a big house, a lot of room for our children. When is the baby coming?"

"About the same time of year that Bohdan was born, Michael. I was so worried about telling you about the baby. I thought you might be angry and I don't like it when you get angry. I think I will have some of the borscht Ann brought over yesterday. Would you like some, Michael?"

Micchael and Helena hugged each other as they walked slowly from the bedside of their dead son to the eating area. So much had happened in such a short time, thought Helena. Is this the way life will go on? Her problems appeared to be so heavy now in comparison to her problems during her days of working for the doctor's wife. That time of Helena's life seemed so long ago but the memories remained, flashing back on her during these times of despair. Life was much easier for her during those years, but our life will get better when we begin farming, Helena assured herself.

TWENTY-SEVEN

Within a few years, Helena had given birth to another four children: three girls and one boy, Rosie, Sophie, Andrew and Emily. Rosie was a frail child in her early years, requiring more sleep than each of the other children. She adapted well at school and seemed to have outgrown her frailness at school age. Sophie, fourteen months younger than Rosie, was a very active child, requiring a great deal of attention from her parents. Andrew arrived earlier than expected, at first becoming a burden for Helena. She was not fully prepared for this addition but did not take long in getting organized. Andrew was content as a baby and toddler, making Helena's days lighter in caring for him. Emily arrived approximately one year following Andrew's birth. She was also a good baby, content to watch Andrew playing. Emily and Andrew spent many hours together each day, becoming playmates as toddlers.

Helena's days were filled with many activities in meeting the day-to-day needs of the family along with developing her skills in sewing. Helena was anxious to attain refinement and mastery that would interest neighbors to pay her a small amount to sew for them. It wasn't long before she had a few jobs that kept her working late into the night when the children were asleep. It was very tiring but she felt rewarded with the money with which she was able to buy material and wool to make clothing for her family. Winters were long and the children needed woolen socks and mittens plus other heavy clothing when they played outside and began walking to and from school. Helena also received used clothing from her sisters for her to take apart, using the material to make more clothing for her family.

During these years, Michael tried different jobs ranging around the sawmill, logging, cutting cordwood and thrashing. He was anxious to have his own land and often talked about the farm deal they missed out on because they didn't have enough money to get started. With the family expanding, it was very difficult to put money away. However, Michael was still hanging on to the small amount he had put away for a down payment. He was looking forward to the day he could purchase a quarter section (160 acres) of farmland.

Helena's brother, Jack, kept visiting her periodically, discussing the possibility of a farming partnership with Michael. Jack's latest plan was, he would spend the next winter working steadily at a camp far up north and expect to earn enough money by spring for his half share of the down payment. Michael did not get too excited about this possibility, but deep down was hoping that by early spring he and Jack would be able to approach the Englishman, Mr. Sand. He had heard that Mr. Sand was not well and was anxious for a sale.

Michael worked in the bush cutting cordwood the winter Jack worked up north. The snow was heavy and the winter extremely cold. At the end of the winter, Michael had not gained much financially and was frustrated.

Helena was very anxious to get her family into a bigger house. Michael and Jacob had added one room to the summer kitchen Helena and Michael were living in, providing a sleeping area for the family. The family was extremely crowded. Helena took on quite a few sewing jobs along with knitting sweaters, scarves, mittens and socks. Helena knew she had to keep this extra work to provide some additional money in order to help Michael begin farming. He was becoming depressed and discontented with his life. Many mornings Helena started another very long day with only a few hours sleep after sewing late into the night. By the end of the winter, Helena was extremely exhausted, and felt worn out, but had a couple hundred dollars hidden away.

TWENTY-EIGHT

Helena and the children were busy preparing for the Easter festivities. Special bread was baked, eggs were decorated and all the family would attend a special service at the church on Sunday morning. Michael would be home prior to the festivities. The children were anxious to have their father home, and each day of the week before his arrival, they were expectantly waiting for him.

On Good Friday, while two of the little children were playing outside, a man on horseback was coming towards them. At first they thought it was their father but after watching him for a while, they recognized their Uncle Jack. "Mama, Uncle Jack is here," they both cried out. "Uncle Jack is here!"

Helena could hear the excitement outside and thought it was Michael home. As she opened the door, she realized it was her brother. "Oh, it's you, Jack, I'm so glad to see you. We are expecting Michael home anytime and I thought it was he. I hope you are going to spend Easter with us."

"Yes, Helena, I will spend a few days with you. I will look after my horse first, and then we can talk. When Michael comes home we can start working on the farm deal. I have enough money for my share in the partnership." Jack spoke with great enthusiasm.

Just as Jack was walking to the house from the barn, in high spirits, he saw Michael walking in from the road. The two children also noticed their father and ran out to meet him. There was much excitement as everyone talked and the children tried to position themselves close to their father and uncle in the house. The children had heard their uncle Jack mention about the farm deal earlier and wanted to know more about it. Michael and Helena were excited that Jack had the cash to join them in this venture. "It is going to be a big Easter celebration, announced Michael. A really big one! We will go on Monday to make a deal with the Englishman."

Mary and Jacob heard the excitement and came over to see what it was all about. At first Mary was upset with the thought of Michael and Helena moving so far away with her family. "I do not want you to live so far away from me, she kept repeating. It means so much to me to have my family close by."

"I know how difficult it will be for all of us, Helena insisted. We have to make a move to get ahead in life and maybe be lucky enough to also get a larger home. We have outgrown this place a long time ago and even with the added room it is too small. If we have more children, I don't know where I will put them. They are sleeping three in a small bed now. The baby is sleeping in our bed. It will soon be time for the oldest child to start school and I am really afraid to send her walking in this bush, with so many bears and other wild animals around. I cannot leave the other children at home alone to walk with Rosie. You have other family members close by. It is important for our family to make the move!"

MICHAEL and HELENA

TWENTY-NINE

I t was at this time in his life when Michael first became a landowner in partnership with Helena's brother, Jack. A down payment was accepted by Mr. Sand, with annual payments to be made in the late fall, following the harvesting. The house was large compared to where Michael and Helena had been living. Helena would have a large kitchen, a parlor, a cellar, plus three bedrooms upstairs.

Helena was extremely happy with the move. She used a small portion of her savings to buy a few used pieces of furniture for the house and some material to sew curtains for the windows. During the first few days following the move, she scrubbed the walls, ceilings and floors as they had been neglected for a while. A coat of paint in some areas would have been a big improvement, but because of restricted finances, this project would hopefully take place the following spring.

Michael and Jack set up farming by purchasing a few heads of cattle, a few horses and the necessary used equipment to work the land. A small area of land close to the house was prepared for the garden, which Helena accepted as her responsibility.

As the summer passed, Michael was experiencing many frustrations. Because of frequent strong, gusty winds and the lack of moisture, the crops were poor and would not yield as much as expected to meet their first payment. Helena kept watering the garden and was able to produce an adequate amount of food for the family. She also raised some chickens, geese, and turkeys, which she expected, would supply the family with meat. However, it looked as though they would be sold for cash to supplement the funds for general maintenance.

When the harvesting was completed and the small amount of grain sold, there was only enough cash to pay a quarter of the annual payment. Helena was able to come forth with the remaining of her savings to pay another quarter of the annual payment. Michael and Jack paid a visit to Mr. Sand and asked for a deferment in the unpaid portion. They promised to have the rest of the money by late winter or early spring. Jack would go to work at the sawmill to earn some money. Michael would tend the cattle and hopefully sell a few heads in the early spring. Mr. Sand accepted the deferment, with a financial penalty.

Several months after Helena had settled into her new home, she realized she was pregnant. She was happy as she felt comfortable in her large home and the two oldest children were now attending school. Another child would not be a problem, she thought to herself. Besides, her neighbors had given her a large box of children's clothing, for all ages. She would have sufficient clothing for the new baby plus some clothing for the other children.

Helena waited until she was four months pregnant before informing Michael of their coming family addition. She hesitated in sharing this information, as Michael had been frustrated with the first year's yield in farming. He kept reiterating his frustrations to her, very concerned as to how they were going to manage. Helena chose one morning after the two oldest children had left for school to break the news to Michael. He was at the kitchen table with the two younger children, chatting to them as they ate their breakfast. He was preparing his bowl of porridge with sugar and milk. "Michael, we will have another child in the spring, around Eastertime," Helena commented. Michael became silent, stirring his porridge but not making any attempt to eat it. "What do you mean by another child, Helena? We can barely make ends meet with the ones we have now. How can we keep making babies without knowing how we are going to provide for them? You told me you were going to be careful. How come you got pregnant?" "Michael, when I try to tell you it is not a good time for lovemaking, you do not pay any attention. If you cannot try to be careful with me, then we will just keep having babies."

Michael ate his porridge in silence then left for the barn. Helena knew in advance Michael was not going to be happy with this announcement and was not surprised at his reactions. He had reacted negatively each time she had informed him of each pregnancy. Why did he blame her? Weren't having children an expectation in marriage? Why will he not accept some responsibility in timing our lovemaking?

THIRTY

The following spring brought a more positive feeling to Helena and Michael. Jack was able to make a good portion of the payment with the money he earned at the sawmill. Michael made up the rest of the payment after the sale of a few cattle. This cleared their debt but did not give them any money for maintenance and any additional equipment, etc. Helena was concerned this situation may occur and prepared herself to the possibility. In the early winter, she approached her neighbors, offering to sew clothing for them at a reasonable price. Her business grew, keeping her very busy and tired but by spring she had enough money put away to cover the cost of the seed, feed for the horses and cattle, and some repairs for the equipment. She also put some money away to cover the cost of a nurse to come to the house to deliver the baby when she was ready for the birth of their child.

The baby, Jane, arrived the day before Easter. Helena felt good having help for the delivery. The nurse cared for Helena and the baby plus the two younger children. Michael kept the two older children occupied with him working outside and in the barn when they were not at school. However, after four days, Helena was on her own, caring for the house and family, with a new baby. Jane was a happy baby as long as she breast-fed frequently. This was time-consuming for Helena. However, she was happy to get some rest, which she needed most at times. Jack and Michael were busy working the land, preparing for seeding plus other required activities, so they were not much help to Helena until after supper. They helped Rosie, the oldest girl, with the dishes while Helena attended to the other children, including breast-feeding the new baby, Jane. During her first two years, Jane had developed into a very active child and was entertaining to her siblings. They loved to include her in their play activities.

Helena loved her family and was happy caring for them but realized the demands were very heavy on her now. Some days she wondered if she could cope with the burdensome workload all day plus being up frequently during the night with the baby. She had very little time to rest, as the garden was also her prime responsibility.

At the end of the summer, Helena's younger sister, Nellie, came to visit for two weeks. She had arranged to attend high school and work for her board and room in Brandon, the city nearby. She had two weeks before school started, so decided to spend this time helping Helena. Helena was very pleased to have Nellie with her. She was good with the children and helped with the housework. The two weeks flew by and Helena felt much more rested following Nellie's visit and assistance. In return, Helena offered to sew a couple of dresses for Nellie for school. Nellie would also spend time with Helena and family during the school holidays. This pleased Helena. She looked forward to the next school holiday, which was Christmas, Nellie arrived for a two-week period at Christmas, enjoying the family environment and her sister's good cooking. One evening, while Nellie was visiting, Helena and Michael had an invitation to attend a neighborhood get—together, approximately four miles from their home. Nellie was happy to spend time alone with the children and encouraged the outing. Michael did not want to take a team of horses and sleigh to travel that evening. The horses had been working most of the day and he needed them to be fresh for the work he was planning the next morning. He chose to harness and hitch a young mare, Fanny, to the stone boat with him and Helena riding on the stone boat. Michael specially built the stone boat for the purpose of hauling stones, using a flat, wooden platform nailed to two wooden runners. The stone boat was light and did not take much strength to pull on the snow when empty. Before leaving the yard, Michael drove around, testing Fanny's reaction to this activity. He felt Fanny had adapted well to pulling the stone boat with him on it, even though it was her first experience. She had pulled the sleigh before with another experienced horse. Michael stopped for Helena in front of the house and they started on their four-mile journey. All went well on the way down, both Michael and Helena had a pleasant ride. They had an enjoyable evening, a rare event to be out without the children. At the gathering Michael sang a number of Ukrainian songs. All present were overwhelmed with Michael's beautiful voice as they listened to him intensely, even though they did not understand the words.

On the way home, Fanny seemed hard to control, as though she was anxious to get home. Michael stood up on the stone boat and kept talking to her, pulling on the reins, trying to calm her down. The faster Fanny traveled, the closer the stone boat would get to the back of Fanny's feet, scaring her. Helena was beginning to worry about how safe they were if Michael could not control Fanny. They were about one mile from home when Helena felt Fanny was becoming wild. Michael continued to pull on the reins but was experiencing great difficulty. He could not control her. Helena thought: What if they had a bad accident and were injured? Who would take care of their children? Helena decided she had to get herself off the stone boat even though Fanny was going at a very fast pace. Helena had brought a quilt with her to keep warm while traveling. She moved herself to the very back of the stone boat, wrapped herself in the quilt, and rolled off. When she stopped rolling and got her bearings, she realized she was not injured. She was on the road and could walk home. Her next big concern was how Michael was doing.

When Fanny arrived close to the barn, she suddenly slowed her pace and headed for the barn door. Michael turned around to talk to Helena and realized she was not there. He expected she must have fallen off, but had no idea how far down the road this could have happened. Michael decided to quickly change to another horse and return to find Helena. She may be injured. Just as Michael pulled out of the long lane and headed on the road, he could see Helena in the distance, walking and dragging her quilt in the snow. He was so happy to see she was not injured. When Michael approached Helena she told him how she rolled off the stone boat. She was afraid they would get thrown off and injured so decided it was safer to roll off. When Michael asked Helena to get on the stone boat and ride home, she refused. She gave him the quilt to take home but preferred to walk. It was an experience that stayed in Helena's memory for a long, long time.

Michael and Jack had a busy summer and fall. They were much more pleased with the crops and had a much higher yield. However, the price of grain dropped in the market and they were short of funds for the second annual payment. They only had enough cash to cover three-quarters of the payment. They had to approach Mr. Sand for a deferment for the second time.

Once again, Jack spent the winter working at the sawmill. Michael had increased the number of milking cows so was hoping to earn some money by selling cream. Michael started out milking the cows but was extremely slow in this process. The cows that were not milked immediately at their appointed times tended to yield a reduced amount of milk. Helena realized the problem and in order to save the milk, took on this added responsibility. At first, she helped Michael and then gradually she was left milking the cows alone while Michael attended to other chores. At times, when the older children were not in the house, she asked Michael to stay with the younger children while she did the milking. In some ways, Helena enjoyed the peace and quietness, away from the family for a while. She enjoyed being deep in thought as she was milking the cows, planning the future for her family, hoping the children would be good students and continue their education at the high school level. This would provide the freedom for each of them to advance in their profession of choice. She would work towards achieving that goal and more, if at all possible, for her children.

THIRTY-ONE

T he next two years brought the same financial results. When harvesting was completed and the grain sold, there was not enough cash to make the payments and for the family living expenses. Jack continued working throughout the winter each year to supplement the income The cream sold by Helena and Michael barely produced enough funds to meet the family's financial needs, mainly for food. At the end of the fourth year, Jack informed Michael he was leaving the partnership and would sign his half of the farm over to Michael. He could not see any point in continuing farming. They were experiencing a depression. Land prices had dropped and they were not gaining in any way. They were getting deeper in debt and would probably end up losing the farm. The depression was affecting most of the families, some had it more severe than others.

Michael was surprised and upset over Jack's decision, but understood his position. The morning Jack spoke to Michael, they had planned on attending an auction sale. Jack informed Michael he would not be attending the auction so Michael headed out on his own. He wanted to look at some seeding equipment required for the next planting in the spring.

Michael sat beside an elderly man during the auction. Michael's mind was really not on the auction bids; he was deep in thought wondering how he was going to handle his financial problems.

When Mr. Reed struck up a conversation, Michael was happy to respond and chat with him.

During the conversation, Mr. Reed indicated he was alone, had no close family, received a small pension, and was looking for a place to live. When the auction sale ended, Michael asked Mr. Reed if he needed a place soon. "Yes, I need a place today and can pay for my board and room upfront," Mr. Reed quickly responded. "Come home with me and you can live with us, Mr. Reed, suggested Michael. We have a few children but I'm sure you will fit in with the family. What about your clothing and possessions?" "Everything I own is in this bag," Mr. Reed stated as he pulled out a gunnysack from under the wooden bench they were sitting on.

Mr. Reed was elated with Michael's positive response. He did not have a home and took a chance by coming to the auction and meeting up with someone that needed funds and would offer him a place to live.

Michael arrived home with Mr. Reed. He was jovial as he introduced Mr. Reed to Helena and the family. Michael's thoughts kept focusing on having some additional funds, not realizing the additional strain and impact a boarder in the home would have on his wife and family.

Helena's first impression when she met Mr. Reed was varied: His clothes needed a good scrubbing and he needed a bath. He needed a haircut and hair wash. His moustache needed trimming. He was wearing those old army uniforms that need to be discarded. They cannot be washed and he probably would not want them dry-cleaned. He seems to be a gruff, old man. How will the children take to him? Where has he been living? What was Michael thinking when he brought this man home? It is more work for me and less sleeping room for the children. I will have to move all the children into the big bedroom and give him the small bedroom.

That night after everyone was settled in, Helena was exhausted. She approached Michael regarding Mr. Reed and questioned how long Mr. Reed expected to be staying. "I told him he could live with us, Helena, replied Michael. This man has a Veteran's pension that he receives each month. The money we receive from him will help feed and clothe the children. Your brother walked out on me so we have to handle all the finances ourselves. I will have to find work away from home this winter and you will have to manage the chores and family on your own. Maybe, Mr. Reed will be helpful in being with the children when you are in the barn, working."

Helena knew they had serious financial problems and would lose their farm if they could not keep up the taxes and payments. Right now, they were in arrears in both tax and farm payments. Where would they go if they lost the farm? She loved her spacious home and did not want to lose it. With a positive attitude, Helena decided to move ahead, accepting the increased responsibilities of having Mr. Reed as a boarder in their home. What else can I do? She thought to herself.

THIRTY-TWO

M r. Reed settled in with the family, spending a great deal of time in his room reading and smoking a pipe. He appeared very gruff to the children and at first they kept away from him. Gradually, he enticed them with candy and they became more comfortable talking to him. Mr. Reed usually ate his meals with the family in the large kitchen but periodically Helena would serve him lunch in his room. She arranged for any available child to assist her in carrying the food to his room. Mr. Reed enjoyed this pampering and praised Helena, making her feel good.

During the winter, the children spent more time directly with Mr. Reed when Helena was involved with the outside chores. He came out of his room, taking charge of the children's activities. Unfortunately, there was pronounced favoritism shown towards one of the girls. This favoritism infuriated the other children, creating a great dislike to Mr. Reed and gradually a dislike towards their sister. The situation continued all during Mr. Reed's stay with the family. He gradually showed a very pronounced negative tolerance to all the children except the one he favored. This created a greater strain among the children. Helena realized there was a problem but was thankful to have an adult in the house with the children while she managed the outside chores, so did not take the children's comments seriously. How could an old man harm the children? Physically, he did no harm but verbally he made threats that frightened them. He also kept his favorite child in his room for long periods. Was there anything to be concerned about? thought Helena. No, I really do not feel good about this man in our home. When Michael comes home in the spring, I will speak to him about my concerns.

When Michael arrived home in the early spring, Helena approached him regarding the situation. "I think Mr. Reed should leave our home, Michael. He is threatening our son, stating that he will chain him down in the cellar. I know Andrew is irritating at times but I do not like what is happening. Andrew is having a few bad dreams, crying out that Mr. Reed is going to catch him and hurt him. We cannot have this going on with the children, Michael."

Michael listened to Helena and assured her he would make some observations now that he was home, and talk to Mr. Reed, if necessary. He felt it was important to keep the old man for financial reasons. "I did not have a full winter's work and earned much less than Jack did when he was here, Michael informed Helena. We will not have enough funds to pay our back payments and buy food. The money I earned will barely cover the costs for the spring planting, feed for the horses and cattle. Helena, talk to the children and make sure they do not aggravate Mr. Reed. Maybe then he will have more tolerance and treat them with more respect."

"Michael, this man is very dirty and I do not like cleaning up after him. His room is filthy and smells terrible from the pipe smoking. He coughs and spits into a pail but misses the pail very frequently. He has a body odor and resents me requesting him to take a bath once a week. I really do not appreciate caring for him and prefer the children not being close to him. I also worry about Emily spending a lot of time with him in his room. I try keeping her out of his room but he calls her back in when I am away from that area."

"Helena, you are imagining evil things. How can you let your mind wander like that? This is an old man and he will not harm anyone, certainly not a child. He has told me many times that he likes our family and has very high praises for you. When

I saw him this morning, he showed me the doll he bought for Emily and will be taking her to the children's beauty contest at the fair this summer. You will have to make her a special dress and make those ringlet curls in her hair. He also mentioned having a photograph taken. I know he cannot do this for all the children, but it is better if one has this opportunity, than none at all. Maybe the other children will have different opportunities."

Helena knew she was not going to win in this discussion. She would have to continue with the present situation, knowing it was not the best for her family. She did try to make a change and that kept her from feeling too distraught. However, deep inside, she did not feel good about having Mr. Reed in their home.

THIRTY-THREE

The next couple of years were a financial disaster for the family. The summers were fueled with extreme winds and heat, with very little rain, burning the earth to a dry powder. Losses were heavy in all grain fields, gardens did not produce sufficient food to last the winter and there was no work in the area for Michael. The depression was difficult to cope with. The price of wheat dropped to thirty-five cents a bushel. Helena gave birth to another child during the winter, a boy they named Alex. This kept Michael from working away from home. Their debt for the farm was far too heavy for him to reduce, even if he did work out all winter. The only thing left for them to do was to remain on the farm until they were evicted, hoping it would not be during the middle of the winter.

Michael received the eviction notice late in the fall. He knew Mr. Sand and his son had increased their cattle herd and would require some assistance that winter. He approached Mr. Sand with a proposal. "I will assist in caring for your herd this winter if you will allow us to remain on the farm for the winter, Mr. Sand. I really do not have any place to take my family, but by spring, will work out something."

Mr. Sand agreed but was concerned about food for the family. "I will speak to the municipality to see if you could receive some food stamps, Michael. It will not be a lot but would buy some basic foods. The neighbors that were not hit heavily with the drought and I will get together to see how we can assist you and your family. I am truly sorry the farming experience was not successful. My wife and I like you and your family very much and are not happy to see you leave but we do not have an alternative. I have held on for you as long as possible."

Michael knew this and was grateful but resented being defeated. Helena was happy to have a home for the winter, but was concerned about the future. Where would they go? When she and Michael talked about their future, she suggested they return to their own people. Maybe they could find a vacant house and fix it up. Michael could return to a sawmill, logging, cutting cordwood. Helena would grow a large garden and perhaps earn some money sewing.

Michael agreed that Helena's suggestion was most practical, but he was not happy returning to that type of work. However, he realized there was no other solution so would go to his family later in the winter and make arrangements for a place to live.

Michael was successful in finding a small vacant home close to the river and not too far from where his parents lived. There would be sufficient water in the river and there was a cleared area for a garden. The children could walk to school with his sister Jean's children, who lived close by.

Helena's two brothers and one sister came with an old truck to help with the move. All the animals and farm equipment had been sold. With part of the money Michael had purchased a car and with this vehicle would transport his family back to his people. He felt good about owning a car and the children were excited about the trip. They were all anxious to be living close to relatives but the children were concerned about communication with their grandparents. Living in an English-speaking community, the children lost some of their ability to speak Ukrainian. Their grandparents continued only in the Ukrainian language. It was going to be a learning experience for the children and grandparents, which Michael was happy about. He wanted the children to be bilingual, just as he and Helena were.

The furniture was tied down on the back of the truck along

with boxes of clothing and other household items. It was agreed that the truck would leave first followed by the family in the car. Hopefully, some of the furniture would be set up in the home before the family arrived. The first part of the journey was exciting for the family and they were looking forward to a reunion with their cousins, aunts, and uncles. The children were a little crowded in the back seat of the car but did not complain. Just as they were reaching the halfway mark of their journey, a loud bang was heard and Michael had difficulty steering the car. "We have a flat tire, Michael angrily informed everyone as he gradually slowed down to a stop at the side of the road. Everybody out of the car while I fix the tire."

Michael had not had much experience with cars and was slow in patching the tube. The children were anxious to get going again and Helena was worried about getting to their destination before dark. What if they have another flat tire, she thought to herself. Fortunately, they made it to Michael's parents place without any further problems. They stayed there overnight, and then went on to settle in their own little home in the morning. As Helena entered the home and looked around, she realized they would be very crowded but was relieved that they would be alone, without the dirty old man playing havoc with her children.

THIRTY-FOUR

M ichael spent the next two years working in the bush, setting aside small amounts of money each week. He was determined to get back into farming and Helena was anxious to have her own home. They enjoyed living close to their relatives and had many enjoyable family get-togethers but could not see a progressive future there. Farming in this area was not possible as the land was heavily populated with trees and bush. In many areas, when you stood on the ground and looked up, you could barely see the sky through the trees. Clearing and developing the land was heavy work and very time-consuming. Farmers were repeatedly experiencing poor crops and had switched to growing hay, mainly feed for their cattle.

Jacob had not progressed in developing the farm. He was able to make both ends meet on his homestead by living very primitively. Mary appeared content in working in her large garden, making comforters and pillows from the feathers of the fowl she raised, butchered and sold. Mary also sold comforters and pillows. Michael learned from Jacob that there were representatives from the government visiting them, questioning Jacob as to why there was not more land cleared, more buildings established. They were given a time frame to show progress. Michael assured Jacob he would communicate with the government and hopefully explain to them the difficult situation the settlers in this area were placed in without the assistance they needed. Michael did not appreciate his father being harassed and threatened by the government. When the inspector came, Michael spoke to him, showed him the heavy wooded areas with swamp, gravel, and stones. Jacob received his deed in the mail a few months later.

After the second winter, Michael set out with the cash savings he had, to buy a quarter section of land he had heard was available at a good price, approximately sixty miles away. The old Nash car was not very reliable but it was the only car he had, so he ventured out with it. "I do not know when I will be back, Helena, but will return as soon as I make a good purchase," he joyfully remarked as he was preparing to leave.

"Providing the car doesn't leave you stranded, responded Helena. Make sure you take lots of patches with you, as those wartime tubes are not very strong and dependable. You won't have the weight of the family in the car so that should be helpful."

Helena and the children anxiously waited for Michael to return. The children had befriended their cousins close by and were not really interested in making another move to a new area. Six days had passed before the children finally saw their father return, driving into the yard. As soon as the car stopped, Michael got out with a big smile on his face, greeting the children. As Helena watched Michael's happy expressions from the house, she was assured he had made a good deal. She had supper ready so she called everyone to come in the house. "Michael, will you tell us all the details at the supper table? We are all anxious to hear how you made out."

As the family was seated around the table, Michael said the blessing and included thankfulness for a business they would be building in the near future. "What do you mean by business, Michael? You went with our savings to buy a farm," Helena responded.

Michael smiled as he filled his plate with perogies. "Yes, Helena, that was my plan, but I ran into some fine people and they directed me to something much better. As I was driving closer towards the farm for sale, I had a second flat tire. This farmer and his wife living close by, Dan and Jenny Lipsak, came to help me and invited me to their home for supper and to stay the night. I accepted, as I did not want to travel at night with the old Nash. During the evening, they talked about the desperate need for a grocery store in their area. People have to travel for miles to a store and some did not have any transportation. If I would consider starting up a business, they would sell me an acre of land at the corner of their property and I could build a store with living quarters at the back. I bought the acre for one hundred dollars and with the rest of the money we can build the buildings and stock the shelves with groceries. Helena, we are going to be storeowners, have a place to live, and have enough land for a large garden. And a new life!"

"What happens if we don't get enough customers, Michael? Did you find out how many people would buy their groceries at a country store? You know people need to go to town to pick up their mail and will probably buy at the larger stores while they are there. If business is not good, we could lose everything again."

"Don't be so negative, Helena. The Lipsaks know what is needed in their area. I really believe that the store will be a good business. Dan has offered to help put up the building and will recruit more men in the neighborhood to help us as well. There is a carpenter I can hire at a cheap rate. I'm going next week to get started and will stay at the Lipsaks' home until our place is advanced far enough for me to live in. Then I will come back for all of you. By then the school term will be finished and the children will be able to get used to the new area and begin at their new school in the fall. The school is one mile away and there's a good road to walk on. Enough talking now, let's finish our supper. These perogies are really good and I would like some more."

Helena really was skeptical about this business venture, but knew she could not change Michael's decision. He was elated, thinking about the future as a country storeowner and anxious to get started. Once again, Helena tried to eliminate the concerned thoughts that had surfaced in her mind, but it was not easy. She tried to envision how they would survive if the business did not work out but could not see any possible alternatives in the plan.

The only thing that kept Helena from her concerned thoughts was that she was busy every minute from early morning until bedtime. When her head hit the pillow at bedtime, Helena was so tired, she went right to sleep. Some nights Helena did not wake up with a child crying. Rosie tried to console her brother or sister and only wake her mother if she was not successful. Helena felt badly about not responding, as she knew Rosie also needed a good nights' sleep.

Helena's first thoughts as she was preparing porridge for breakfast in the morning for the next few days was, Will this store gradually become my responsibility? I can barely cope with all of the workload now. What was Michael thinking when someone named Mrs. Lipsak talked him into this venture? She probably thought a store would be a convenience for her as it was a long way to travel to a store from her place. I will find out more when I meet these people but it is too late to make a change.

THIRTY-FIVE

Michael spent approximately three months away from the family, digging a well and getting the building up on the newly acquired one-acre land. With the help of a couple of women in the neighborhood, he also planted a garden. The garden was growing well but needed weeding—a chore he definitely was not fond of and not used to performing. He was anxious to get the family moved in to hand over the responsibility of the garden to Helena. He also was anxious to have the family settled with him and get his business started. Michael's diet consisted mainly of bread and bologna or garlic sausage, plus some raw vegetables from the garden. He could hardly wait for Helena's delicious meals being prepared for him.

It was a sunny, warm day when the family made the journey to their new home. The children were excited about living in a home with a grocery store. Would they be able to serve the customers? Would there be candy in the store? Helena had mixed emotions during the journey to her new home and new life. Her biggest concern was whether the store would produce enough funds for the family to live on.

As they drove closer to the area of the store, Michael pointed out and named the farmers who had been instrumental in assisting him with digging the well and constructing the building. When they drove into the yard of the store and house, Jenny Lipsak was sitting on the front step, waiting for them. She introduced herself before the family could get out of the car. "Michael, I was anxious to meet your family and am preparing supper for all of you. The children can come over sooner while you get set up. I see a truck coming now, is it bringing your furniture and belongings?"

"Thank you, Jenny, Helena responded. I need some of the children to help me. I think it is best if they all stay here. We expected the truck to arrive before us. We will all work together, unload the truck and car, then will be happy to join you later for supper, if that is all right with you."

Helena was anxious to see their new living quarters and preferred not to have snoopy neighbors around during her initial viewing. The building behind the store looked small to her, smaller than the little house they vacated. As soon as Jenny left, Helena walked over to the store, entering slowly. She was pleasantly surprised with the shelves built around most of the wall space and a large counter along one side with the weighing scale sitting on one end. The door at the back entered into their living quarters, a two-room home for all eight of them. This is going to be crowded, she thought to herself as she looked around the room. I guess I can get two double beds and a single bed in the smaller room. The pullout in the bigger room will also be used for sleeping. It is too bad Michael didn't build me some shelves like he did in the store but maybe he will later.

In a short time, Helena was ready for the truckload of their possessions, directing her two youngest brothers in setting up the beds, stove, table, and benches. Before leaving for supper with the Lipsaks, she felt somewhat settled in her new home. She prepared a lunch for her brothers before they returned with the truck they had borrowed from their neighbor.

During the evening at the Lipsaks, Helena was not as comfortable as Michael appeared to be. There was something about Jenny that she did not particularly like, a nosey, dominant streak. In Helena's opinion, Jenny gave her the impression that she was doing them a favor by allowing them a store and residence on their property. The next morning she expressed her concerns to Michael but he just laughed at her, stating she was imagining things. In his opinion, Jenny was just being helpful to them and wanted to be a good friend and neighbor.

Michael and Helena worked steadily getting their store and home established. Business was building up gradually and Michael was enjoying the lifestyle. He made the customers comfortable, displaying an outgoing, pleasant personality. The English families were impressed with his English diction and writing. In order to compete with the larger stores, Michael had to consent to credit, mainly to the farmers. At first there was no risk as the debts were paid up, mostly following harvest. Gradually, these debts were carried for longer periods and Michael was running into financial problems over fresh capital for restocking the groceries. During this crucial time, Helena's brother Jack approached her to care for his two-year-old child, Orest, on a full-time basis. Jack's wife was very young and had left Jack and her son. Jack wanted to go to Duncan, British Columbia, to work. Jack would pay Helena a small sum each month for the care of Orest, plus extra funds for clothing as required. Helena knew in her heart there really was not room in her home for another child, and she did not have time to care for another child. Because the child's mother had left him, and other family members had refused to care for him, she would feel guilty if she refused. "My nephew needs a home and my brother was good to us when we farmed together," she rationalized during her discussion with Michael. I think we should take Orest. He will be company for our youngest son, Alex. The extra money will also help us until some of these debts are collected."

The children responded well to the family addition. They were happy to have their young cousin live with them. He was a happy, loving child. During his toddler years, the girls were anxious to take turns caring for him and Orest blended into the family well. He loved the attention and activity around him.

A COUNTRY STORE

THIRTY-SIX

The general country store business did not expand as Michael had anticipated. As soon as Michael tried to collect on the debts owing, many of these customers discontinued buying from him. His collection success rate was low, plus he lost many customers.

Helena worked diligently earning a little money on sewing projects for neighborhood families. This profit also gradually decreased as families went elsewhere to shop for their groceries. She was extremely upset with the situation, wondering how they were going to exist. Michael was spending each harvest, working on a steamer that fed the threshing machine. He spent approximately six weeks working in the area, away from home most of the time. That left Helena with the responsibilities of the store, home, family and garden during this period. The oldest girl Rosie was taking the first year of high school by correspondence with the help of the teacher at the one-room public school that all the children attended. In order to continue her schooling, she would have to attend the high school in town. There was no bus service so she would have to live in town. How could they afford to send her on to school? Helena kept thinking, as she worked away day after day with this on her mind.

Halfway through the summer school holidays, Helena discussed this issue with Michael but was not satisfied with his response, just as she had experienced when this issue was previously discussed. "Michael, we will have to make some arrangements for Rosie to attend high school in town, "Helena stated.

"Why? She doesn't need any more education to be a wife and mother, Michael responded. That is the role expected of the girls. Besides, we do not have the funds for education. You have been doing very well without high school education, haven't you?"

"But Rosie is a good student and wants to go on to school, Michael. She wants to be a teacher. She doesn't have to spend her life the same way I have. I spoke with Mrs. Bilow yesterday and she has given me the name of a lady in town that takes a student to live with her and the student helps her in return for board and room. I would like to talk to this lady."

"I am sorry, Helena; it is beyond us to provide further education for our children. We cannot do anything more than what is available at our school. Rosie will have to get a job working for some farm lady or town lady until she gets married, just like the other girls do around here. Maybe you could use some help while I go out to work. It looks as though I will have to join the Army or go to work in the mines. My cousin John says there is work in the mine where he is up north."

Helena knew they could not help their daughter financially, but she also was determined to do everything in her power to educate her daughter and the rest of her family. She would not keep Rosie at home to help her with the family chores. Early the next morning, after the milking chores were completed, Helena decided she would walk to town and talk to this lady about a room for Rosie where she could possibly work for her board and room.

It was a long way to walk, but Helena got an early morning start, shortly after sunrise, and was at Mrs. Jackson's house by noon. She was fortunate in getting a ride the last couple miles with a farmer hauling some squealing pigs to town for shipping. He let Helena off at the train station, not far from Mrs. Jackson's house. The farmer was aware of Helena's situation, her long walk home, and offered her a ride back with him, to his turn off. That would leave her only four miles to walk home. Helena anxiously and thankfully accepted. He would be leaving in about two hours, after the pigs were loaded on the boxcar at the train station. He asked Helena to meet him at the train station in two hours. Helena was pleased that her walk home would be reduced immensely. Her feet and legs were sore from her walk this morning. The smell on the wagon from the pigs was heavy, but gradually would reduce with the wind blowing, Helena thought to herself. It was much better than walking.

Helena was nervous and anxious as she knocked on Mrs. Jackson's door. She knew her clothing was soiled with perspiration, her shoes showed signs of wear with a few prominent holes over her bunion areas, and she was possibly carrying the odor of pigs on her clothing. Helena felt weary and hungry, but as Mrs. Jackson greeted her at the door, a feeling of warmth and caring passed through her body, making her feel good. Helena immediately liked this lady. She seemed understanding and eager to help.

"Helena, let us first sit down and have some lunch and tea. You have come a long way and I'm sure you must be hungry. Mrs. Jackson took Helena by the arm to a big comfortable chair while chatting with her. You rest for a few minutes while I prepare some lunch in the kitchen." Helena was happy to sit back in the chair and close her eyes. She must have fallen asleep. Helena woke up when Mrs. Jackson entered the room with a big tray of sandwiches and tea.

Helena informed Mrs. Jackson that she had received a ride all the way into town with her husband. Observing Helena closely, Mrs. Jackson felt this woman had walked a long distance. In Mrs. Jackson's assessment, Helena presented herself as being determined and supportive in educating her daughter. Helena readily drank the tea and ate the sandwiches as they talked, but did not include her husband in the discussions.

"You say you have no money but your daughter could work for her board and room, Helena. I have a girl, Ruth, with me now in that position. Do you have a large garden?"

"Oh yes, Mrs. Jackson. I feed my whole family with my

garden vegetables and still have extras. Could I supply you with vegetables?"

"I have an idea, Helena. There is a room in the attic that is not in use. It has a single bed and could be fixed up for your daughter. If you would like to have the room in return for vegetables from your garden, we have a deal. Ruth will be finished with high school next year, so Rosie can take her place working for her board and room, if she plans to continue her schooling."

"Yes, Mrs. Jackson. I will take your offer and thank you so much. I'm so grateful that my Rosie will be going on to school. She wants to be a teacher. I sure do thank you again. Rosie will be so happy."

Helena displayed happiness, thinking pleasant thoughts as she rode, then walked the remainder of the miles home. She was extremely pleased with the outcome for her daughter but wondered how she would get the vegetables to Mrs. Jackson. I guess I'll worry about that later, she thought. Something will hopefully turn up.

On entering the yard as Helena returned home, she heard loud voices coming from the store. She recognized Jenny Lipsak's voice screaming, "You get out! You get out!" Concerned, she went directly to the store, faced by very angry neighbors, Jenny and Dan Lipsak. Michael was standing behind the counter equally as angry, but saying nothing.

"What is going on here? Why are you yelling?" Helena asked Jenny.

"I want you off my property," Jenny shouted. "But this is our property," Helena responded. "We bought this acre of land from you."

"You tell her, Michael," Jenny continued as she walked out the door, followed by her quiet husband.

"Michael, tell me what is going on here? What is this lady talking about?"

Michael took a deep breath and tried to compose himself. "Jenny is trying to get us off this property. She says we do not own it because we do not have a deed. It is true, Helena, we do not have a deed. I bought this acre of land for one hundred dollars and I shook hands with both Jenny and Dan after we made the deal. We agreed not to hire a lawyer to draw up the deed, as it would be expensive. Now Jenny says they will hire a lawyer to get us off the property. Dan just goes along with her. He doesn't say a word."

Michael and Helena both felt exasperated. They looked at each other, trying to find a vision of hope. It seemed the world kept turning to bleaker moments, defusing any rays of sunshine for them. "I'm going to see the children and prepare some supper, Michael. Maybe after supper we can talk."

Helena left Michael in the store and stepped into their home with exhaustion and tears in her eyes. She tried to put on a happy face for the children by quickly thinking of her success in arranging for Rosie to continue her education.

Helena called the children together, informing them of her experience in town. Rosie was peeling potatoes for supper and quickly stopped after her mother finished talking, gave her mother a big hug and yelled out, "I am going to be a teacher! I am going to be a teacher! How will you get the vegetables to Mrs. Jackson, Mom?"

"I really don't know, replied Helena, but you know our saying, *Where there's a will, there's a way.* I'm going to go that route. "

THIRTY-SEVEN

In the fall, Michael and Helena's oldest daughter, Rosie, initiated the trend of continuing education in their area, as she began her first year attending high school. Helena felt proud when she talked to Mrs. Bilow, thanking her for assisting her in finding a place for Rosie to live during the school term. Michael left for work up north in the mines shortly after school began. Helena battled with Jenny on an ongoing basis, as she managed the store and family. In Helena's eyes, Jenny reminded her of a witch. She had a mean streak, constantly harassing her and the children. Helena was determined not to give in to this mad lady. Jenny wasn't long in visiting the neighboring farmers, informing them that the store would soon be closing and that the family would be moving as soon as Michael got a place for them to live up north.

Business at the store was down to a snail's pace. People came mainly because of curiosity, purchasing very little. Helena knew this and said very little to them when questioned, except that the store was not closing. However, stock was noticeably down and Helena could not place an order unless she paid cash. There had been consistent delays in paying for the last few orders, placing the store on the poor credit rating list. Michael was working steadily and saving money. If he could continue in the mines for a couple years he would have enough money to buy a farm, he informed Helena in his letters. He encouraged Helena to keep the store going as long as possible and he would come home for a holiday after 18 months of work. Maybe then they could decide how to proceed.

Helena was kept very busy and tried avoiding Jenny. It was difficult as Jenny lived close by and watched for Helena to go outdoors. She would then come out and harass Helena verbally as soon as she saw her outside. "You are on my property. I want you off my property. Where is that husband of yours?" Jenny called out. Helena decided it was best not to respond to Jenny's comments. She began ignoring her. This silence from Helena agitated Jenny and she became louder and louder. Gradually the neighbors became more sympathetic to Helena's situation with Jenny and Dan. They tried discouraging Jenny in pursuing this harassment and evacuation of a sincere, good living family. They were not successful. Jenny became obsessed with anger and rage towards Helena and Michael, verbally attacking any family member at every opportunity. She made negative comments about Helena's pursuit in educating Rosie.

Educating Rosie kept Helena's morale up. She sent vegetables to Mrs. Jackson with a neighbor whenever it was possible, but the times became less frequent. She was aware she was not fully carrying out her end of the bargain. Would this kind lady continue to keep her daughter? Fortunately, Mrs. Jackson took a liking to Rosie and before the end of the school term, arranged for her to return in the fall and work for her board and room. Both Helena and Rosie were elated and thankful to this very kind lady.

"Why does Mrs. Lipsak yell at us all the time? The children frequently questioned Helena. We do not know what she is saying in the Polish language, but we know she is angry and does not like us. The two daughters will not play with us at school. They will not respond when we talk to them."

Helena suggested to the children that they try to understand Mrs. Lipsak. "She is not well and becomes angry very quickly. Because we live close by, she takes her anger out on us. It is best that you ignore her. Your dad will be buying a farm as soon as he has earned and saved enough money. Then we will be able to move away from this lady and hopefully have some peace. She upsets me very much, but I cannot do anything to stop her. Legally, Mr. and Mrs. Lipsak own this land we are living on. Your dad paid for it but did not get a deed. Without a legal deed we cannot fight them. It is a very unfortunate situation for us. It will soon be winter. With the doors and windows closed, we won't hear the yelling as much. Maybe by spring this angry lady will cool down."

THIRTY-EIGHT

I t seemed like a long two years before Michael returned home with his savings, ready to purchase a farm. The savings were sufficient to purchase a quarter section of undeveloped land, which he did. He would have to return to the mine to earn funds for clearing the land and to buy equipment for farming. This meant being away from the family for another long period of time.

Helena felt trapped, working long hours into the night, meeting the needs of the family. She felt somewhat relieved when Michael purchased the quarter section of land, knowing there was a place to move the buildings to, even though the land was all bush, with many stones. It was their very own property. After many years of hardship and frustration, Michael finally became a paid-up landowner, making sure he had a legal deed to the property.

By spring, the pressure from Jenny was extremely heavy. Helena decided she could not wait for Michael to come home and move the buildings. She arranged with several neighbors and friends to have the buildings, contents, two cows and chickens moved to the farm, located five miles away. The move went well and the children were delighted with the vast area of land. They were anxious to roam in the woods and explore their new territory.

In order to move the buildings, the one-room store was detached from the two-room house, leaving an open area on the house. Each building was pulled by a tractor on the dirt road and relocated in a small cleared area on the farm. The men involved in the move stated they were unable to place the buildings close enough to re-attach when relocated. They were set up separately, in close proximity, with an open area on one side of the house. Helena prayed for the rain to hold off until she could arrange for a neighboring carpenter to close in this area. In the meantime she hung some blankets over the opening to keep the wind, dirt, and flies out as much as possible.

Living on the farm was very primitive, with many unavailable necessities, including a well for water, a cool area for storing food, a toilet, etc. Water was carried in pails from a small stream on the property. The cows also drank from the stream. Helena was concerned the stream would dry up if there were not sufficient rains. Fortunately, the stream kept them supplied with water. Helena boiled the water before using it in the home. The wood for the stove had to be obtained by cutting down trees with an axe, sawing the logs in sections, then splitting them into smaller pieces with an axe. There was no transportation. The older children walked approximately four miles each way to the village for the mail and food supplies. They tried to get a ride home or partway home with a neighbor whenever possible. A small area of land close to the house was cleared by the men in the neighborhood and cultivated for planting vegetables. Helena was very happy to be able to plant a garden and was very thankful to the men in the neighborhood for all the help they had extended her and her family. She expressed her thanks to each of them and was very much taken aback by the comments from one man. "With your husband away, Helena, maybe I could be helpful to you sexually?" Helena could not believe what she was hearing. She walked away from this man in anger, without responding. Why would this man even think of such behavior? She thought to herself. I am a wife and mother with many responsibilities; right now sex is furthest from my mind. Helena decided she would not tell Michael this detail, as it would only cause friction between the two men. She hoped they would not have much contact with this family in the future.

Michael continued working in the mine for another few months. He would have continued for a longer time but Helena needed help: A barn for the cows and chickens needed to be built before the winter; a well had to be dug for water before the frost was in the ground; a cellar needed to be dug under part of the house to store the vegetables for the winter. Helena could have used the money from Michael's work for the family, but was not able to cope on her own with the needs on the farm. The two eldest children had arranged to continue their high school education by working for their board and room in town; they would not be home to help her in the fall. Helena missed the help from the children but was thrilled to know they were able to continue their high school education.

THIRTY-NINE

There was an expectation in this farming community that all children should contribute to family chores—land development, farm work and housework—at a young age. Some children were kept home from school for this purpose, affecting their ability to maintain their grades. Fortunately, Helena did not totally support this concept and expectation. She encouraged all of her children to attend school regularly. Knowing that they had their mother's support, the girls were very strong in pursuing the goal for continuing their education, even though it was very difficult for them. Firstly, there was not a high school located in the rural areas or bus service to a high school. Secondly, there was no financial assistance available to them and their father, along with most fathers in the neighboring areas, did not support education for their daughters beyond public school.

With the help and support of Helena, each of her children moved out of the nest to attend high school, plus obtain further education. The girls worked at low-income housekeeping jobs during the summer holidays to earn sufficient funds to pay for the books required for the next term.

Emily kept thinking about her high school education and her early working experiences. She took her first-year of high school by correspondence at the school she and her siblings had attended before moving to the farm. The distance walked each way from the farm was two and one-half miles. The other children attended a school closer to their home, but Helena felt the teacher at the previous school was more experienced and would be more helpful to Emily. It was a positive experience for Emily, thanks to Helena.

After Emily completed grade nine, Michael and Helena suggested that she skip a year to help her mother at home while her father was away working at the mines during the winter. Emily believed helping her mother for one year while her father was working in the mine would be a very challenging experience and a contribution by her to the family. It made her feel important. However, her thoughts were very strong to continue her education the following year. Helena depended on Emily to handle the outside and barn chores, including caring for, harnessing, and driving the newly acquired horses. Emily was petrified of these two very fast bronco horses and had not cared for them while her father was home. She would not admit these fears to her mother, as she knew her mother was not comfortable with horses, too. Emily decided she would work with them slowly and gradually become more competent and comfortable managing them. Emily thought back to the first time she harnessed, hitched and drove the horses to the village, approximately four miles away, for Helena to obtain the necessities from the store and pick up the mail. Helena preferred her to leave home after an early supper so that they could receive the mail coming in on the train at 9:30 P.M. Emily was petrified as the horses scared easily and were hard to control, more so at night. Fortunately, there was a bright moon shining that evening and there were no problems. It was a challenge and relief to get back home, the horses unhitched, unharnessed, fed and watered, without any incident.

Another outstanding task Emily remembered her mother had challenged her with was to butcher a rooster for the family Sunday dinner. This turned out to be a disaster for Emily. She made several attempts to chop off a rooster's head but was not successful. Each time she brought the hatchet down, the rooster moved its head on the block and a wing got clipped. A neighbor heard of their situation and offered his assistance. This was very much appreciated by the family as fowl was their only available meat at that time of year.

When spring arrived, Emily started looking for summer work to earn money for books for the fall school term. She was delighted to be interviewed by a family approximately 40 miles away. The family lived on a prosperous farm and had two children—the third child was to be born in August. Emily's responsibilities would include caring for the two children, helping out with the housework, gardening, and milking. She would earn fifteen dollars per month for two months. That suited Emily, as she needed the money.

Emily recalled vividly her enthusiasm in getting ready to go with these people. She was astonished when she looked over at her mother and saw tears rolling down her mother's face as she watched Emily pack her few clothes. Emily wondered at the time why her mother was crying, thought she was being helpful to her mother by trying to be independent. Not until Emily became a mother herself did she realize the feelings one experiences as your child leaves the nest. She has relived those moments many times, understanding how difficult it must have been for her mother to let her go, knowing the expectations and responsibilities Emily would be facing.

Emily related to her first job as a challenge. She worked long hours, beginning at 5:30 A.M., trying to blend in with the family responsibilities: milking six cows each morning, separating the milk from the cream through a separator, washing the separator utensils and milking pails. She continued through the day caring for the children, helping with the housework, attending to the needs in the garden, working until bedtime. During one period in the summer, she was left alone with these responsibilities while the mother was admitted to the local hospital for the birth of their third child.

Emily learned the procedure for shelling peas by using the washing machine wringer. The washing machine wringer consisted of two rubberized rollers on springs, rotated with a hand crank. The function of the wringer was to remove as much water as possible from the clothing after each washing and rinsing, by placing the clothing between the two rubberized rollers. In the pea shelling procedure, the peas in the pods are placed between the rollers. When the pod reaches the roller, it splits, allowing the peas to fall into a container. The pods go on between the rollers, falling into another container on the other side of the wringer. Emily was very cautious not to get her fingers caught in the wringer. The washing machine and wringer were new experiences for Emily, as Helena did not have this equipment; she used a scrub board to wash the clothes.

Emily was very lonely for her family while she was working but would not admit to it in the letters she wrote to them. She wanted so much to be successful in her life and realized this was the beginning of her adult development. By the time evening rolled around each day, she was exhausted and ready for bed. The mornings seemed to arrive in no time and Emily wondered what it would be like to sleep in. Her most encouraging time never to be forgotten was when Helena telephoned her one day to ask how she was getting along. Emily was so elated that her mother was thinking of her but felt guilty and sad as she knew her mother would have had to walk a few miles to a telephone to call her. Until her mother's call, Emily really felt nobody was interested in how she was doing; her employers were just interested in how well she was able to perform in assisting them in their needs. Emily knew then that her mother really cared about her and she was looking forward to purchasing Helena a gift with part of her earnings at the end of the summer.

At the end of the first month, Emily received fifteen dollars for her work. She hid the money in the pocket of a pair of slacks in the dresser drawer. This was sufficient money for the purchase of her books for the next school year. She would not be able to spend any of her earnings for anything other than books and clothing. She was badly in need of a winter coat. Her old one was small on her. Helena had altered the sleeves and length of the coat last year. Emily did not like wearing the coat as the new length of the sleeves and coat were a much darker color than the rest of the coat.

At the end of the second month, Emily was approached by her employer, for her to accept two dresses plus five dollars for her work. These dresses fit Emily and looked good on her, but they were summer dresses, not what she required for school. However, Emily had difficulty refusing the offer. She purchased a tablecloth for her mother and went home with less money than she had planned on, realizing she would have to wear her winter coat another winter.

When Emily arrived home from her summer job, a very upset family greeted her. Alex and Orest were crying. Wiping his tears, Alex informed Emily that Orest would be leaving their home to live with his dad, beginning the following week. Orest's dad had purchased a local grocery store with a small, attached home in the local village and Orest would be moving in with him. Emily had realized this change in their family would probably occur in time, but she was not aware it would be so soon. The family had Orest for eight years and now it was time for them to let go, time for Orest to get to know his dad. Orest needed his dad and his dad needed him. Emily made an effort to make the transition a happy and exciting occasion by presenting a positive attitude towards the situation. Alex felt he was losing a brother and friend. Orest felt sad about leaving the family but was excited about his new life with his dad. Emily assured Alex he and Orest would be able to visit frequently. Fortunately, time heals and with frequent visits at the beginning, adjustments were made. Alex and Orest continued a close relationship.

FORTY

After completing her summer job, Emily went to see the principal of the high school in town, asking if he knew of a family interested in having a student work for their board and room while attending high school. She told him how she wanted to complete sufficient requirements for entrance into nursing school, but her parents could not assist her financially. Mr. Cook, the principal, responded that he might know someone interested and asked Emily to return to his home in an hour. Emily went for a walk around town, passing the high school, fantasizing and hoping she would be fortunate in attending the school the following week.

When Emily returned to Mr. Cook's home, he was waiting for her, along with his wife and three children. Mr. Cook introduced Emily to his family. He stated he had a home for Emily for the school term period. She could live at his home with his family and help his wife with the children after school and weekends. Unfortunately, the house was small and Emily would have to sleep on the couch in the living room. Emily was surprised with this offer and felt good about her opportunity to be living with the principal's family, even though she did have to sleep on the couch. She was used to sharing a bed with her two sisters, so she had been looking forward to sleeping alone. She quickly made up her mind to accept the offer.

The first few weeks at the Cooks' home was enjoyable. Emily

related well with the children and was spending a great deal of her time with them each day after school. She worked on her homework after washing up the supper dishes, before making her bed on the couch for sleeping. Mr. and Mrs. Cook went to bed early, and Mr. Cook initiated his day early in the morning by reading and working on class preparations, using the kitchen area.

Peculiar incidents started happening to Emily in the early hours of the morning. She felt something crawling around her under the blanket. It was dark and she envisioned a mouse in her bed. She had experienced a mouse in her bed when sleeping in the granary at home during the summer. When Emily kicked and turned in bed, it went away. This incident happened a few mornings. She did not want to mention the situation to the Cooks, thinking it may disturb them. One morning, Emily opened her eyes when this peculiar incident was taking place again and saw Mr. Cook, the principal, bending over her with his right hand under her blanket. She could not believe what was happening. Mr. Cook immediately stood up straight with a smile on his face, stating he came to waken her to get ready for school. Even though it was a little early, he thought she might like to spend some time on her studies. It was far too early in the morning to be woken but Emily did not say anything. She was stunned! Her school principal, a husband and father of three children, was attempting inappropriate actions in his own home, with her, his student. She decided to get up and go for a walk before Mrs. Cook and the children woke up. How was she going to continue living in this home, plus attend classes taught by this man? she kept thinking to herself. She wondered if Mrs. Cook was aware of her husband's conduct. This was an issue Emily felt she could not discuss with anyone but realized she needed to move out of this home. She felt her parents would not be supportive to her, unable to believe this conduct from a school principal. Her father would be under the impression that Emily encouraged this man. It would be embarrassing to tell her friends at school. Mr. Cook, being High School Principal, was well respected in the town. Would they believe her? Emily decided it was best if she did not speak to anyone regarding the incident. She desperately wanted to continue her schooling and would not allow this man to prevent her from achieving her goal. She would try to find another place to live as soon as possible and would remain with this family until she was successful in relocating. Emily also developed a plan as to how she would handle any future inappropriate actions from her principal. She would scream as loud as she could if he touched her. That would bring attention to the situation. Fortunately, there were no further incidents while Emily remained in this home.

Emily was able to arrange work in exchange for her board and room in another home, this time with an elementary school teacher and family consisting of two children, ages six and seven. The children's father was in the military service and lived at the military camp, coming home periodically for visits. Emily lived with this family until she completed her high school education while caring for the children, helping prepare meals, cleaning up after meals and cleaning the home on weekends. She was required to return to the home as soon as the classes were over, supervise the children, and begin preparing supper. The children's mother stayed at the school until later, preparing her lessons for the next day. A number of Emily's classmates met at a local restaurant after school for a Coke and chat. They frequently asked her to join them. When Emily declined, they did not seem to understand her position in having regular responsibilities and yet having no money for a Coke. Emily was not comfortable with many of her classmates as their lifestyles and responsibilities were so different from hers.

Emily experienced a tremendous burden attending classes taught by Mr. Cook. She had lost total respect for this man and, in fact, hated him. Mr. Cook frequently approached Emily in class with a smile on his face, asking how she was managing in her new home and whether she had sufficient time for her studies. Emily did not make good grades but was successful in completing the necessary education to be accepted into nursing school

The true reason for leaving the Cooks' home was not revealed to Emily's family until Emily married and had children of her own. When Emily explained the situation to her mother, Helena responded with hostility. Helena admired individuals with advanced education but she had difficulty accepting the fact that these people would not always function at an acceptable standard and would take advantage of a situation. These individuals had problems, which had an impact on many people, including their own family members.

FORTY-ONE

At the age of sixteen, Emily had sufficient qualifications to enter nursing school but did not meet the requirement age of eighteen. Teachers were very much needed in rural schools at this time, and opportunities were made available for high school graduates to obtain permits to teach for one year by attending normal school for six weeks during the summer. Emily's mother encouraged Emily to enter this program and consider teaching as a profession. The teaching program required less time as a student compared with nursing's. This was a plus in her mothers' thinking.

Emily enrolled in the teaching program and became a permit teacher for one year in a rural school with twenty-nine children from grades one to seven. One student in the seventh grade was very close to her age. Emily was concerned about this factor initially but soon she realized it did not present a problem. This student was a big support to her. Emily used her public school teacher as a role model and followed this teacher's teaching format. It proved to be a very successful approach.

Emily felt the teaching experience was a benefit to her growth and development, providing her with a feeling of worthiness plus respect from her students and the community. Because of her primitive and financially poor background, Emily had remained quiet and shy, lacked confidence and never really became close to her peers. As a teacher, her life changed. She enjoyed the feeling of having an identity and being recognized as an equal, contributing individual. Emily was able to purchase a new wardrobe, was popular in dating, and was saving money for nursing school.

Emily's mother was hoping that Emily would change her mind about nursing and continue instead her education in the teaching profession. However, Emily had a strong desire to become a registered nurse. Although she enjoyed the experience in teaching, it was not her profession to pursue. Actually, Emily would have loved to consider professional dancing as her career. This urge was discounted early in her life, knowing it was an unachievable goal.

Her teaching experience coming to a close soon, Emily had seven months to prepare for nursing school. She decided to utilize this time exploring the possibility of obtaining employment in the city. Fortunately, an aunt living in the city was most generous in sharing her home with family members. Emily and several of her sisters took advantage of this opportunity, enjoying many of the facilities not available to them at home in the farm.

Emily took her first job as a waitress at a soda fountain. This type of work and recognition was totally different from what she had recently as a teacher. On the fourth day of her employment, a customer threw a cup of coffee at her because she did not respond to him as quickly as he anticipated. Emily was busy serving another customer. The employer did not deal with the customer on Emily's behalf. She felt humiliated—frustrated— as she tried to soothe the burning sensation on her body from the hot coffee with cool, wet cloths.

When Emily returned home that day, her aunt encouraged her to seek employment elsewhere, which she did. Emily did not go back to the soda fountain and did not get paid for her four days of work. She felt very much abused by this incident but did not have the courage to speak out for her rights. Her employer did not believe she had any rights. In his opinion, the customer is always right.

Emily's next employment experience was at Eaton's Catalogue sales office. The customer spent time viewing the catalogue and placed their order with the salesclerk. The salesclerk made the necessary arrangements for the customer to view the merchandise. A runner obtained the merchandise. Emily functioned as one of these runners. Should the customer purchase the merchandise, the salesclerk completed the order. Should the merchandise not be purchased, it was the responsibility of the runner to return the merchandise to the appropriate area. In case large sized merchandise could not be brought out for viewing, the runner escorted the customer inside for a firsthand look.

Emily was extremely flustered one day when she had to escort her school inspector, Mr. Peach, and his wife, to a specific area for merchandise viewing. Mr. Peach recognized Emily immediately and wanted to know what she was doing in this line of work. Mr. Peach praised Emily's teaching; he indicated to her that she performed well and had great potential in the teaching profession. Emily informed him of her plan to enter nursing school, but that there was an unexpected delay. Mr. Peach reiterated his praise for her teaching and encouraged her instead to continue her education in the teaching profession.

FORTY-TWO

Helena made every attempt possible to support each child as they reached out into the world. She let them know of her concerns: Her comments frequently expressed were, "There is nothing here for you to make a living. You need to get some education and go where there is a better opportunity for you; I have no money to help you, but I will not hold you back."

Michael continued in believing that women do not need so much schooling to become educated. He gave no support to his daughters and was not inclined with providing any assistance for them. In his opinion, girls were meant to be wives and mothers and did not require an education; they learned all they needed to know from their mothers. Helena differed constantly with Michael regarding this issue and was determined her daughters would have an easier life than she and other women in her area have had. She kept plugging away, very proud to be a part of her family's educational challenges, despite Michael's negative attitude.

Michael had made so much progress in learning the English language and was keeping himself fluent in the Ukrainian tongue. He functioned as an interpreter for relatives and neighbors who had not adapted to the English language. He was well respected for these skills. Michael also enjoyed performing and singing in the Ukrainian language. Whenever there was an opportunity, he offered to participate and was recognized as a local actor in the

Ukrainian language. He was very happy during these practices and performances.

The farmland purchased by Michael was not easy to develop and there were many stones. It was not a productive endeavor. Michael spent a great deal of time working in the mines, planning to build a new home with some of his earnings. Helena did not mind managing the farm with the help of the children, knowing she would be achieving by having a new home in the future.

When Michael left the mines and returned home, he was hesitant about building a new home, telling Helena it was not necessary. His reasoning for this decision was, They managed in two rooms with a large family for many years: Why did they need more space now, particularly when many of the children no longer lived at home?

Helena felt there was no point arguing with her husband, decided she would go to the city and get a job, and left Michael with the two youngest children to manage on his own. She had spent her lifetime working, hoping to improve their lifestyle. So many years had passed by and she could not see any improvements.

Helena went to Winnipeg and lived with her sister and family there. She was hired immediately in a sewing factory, paid by the number of items completed by her each day, in an arrangement called piecework. This was a challenge to Helena. She was a fast sewer—very accurate—and she earned a good salary each week. Helena immediately sent parcels of clothing to the two children at home. She missed her home and family very much. The children were elated with the new clothing but were very lonely for their mother. Michael was also having a difficult time coping with the housework. He tried baking bread but was not very successful. He was not knowledgeable in maintaining the home. It really was a disaster. After several weeks Michael wrote to Helena, asking her to return home. Helena thought about his request, responded that she would return, providing Michael built the home that he promised her. Michael agreed and in time, after overcoming many frustrations, Michael and Helena became owners of a new home on the farm, with two bedrooms, a kitchen, living room and dining room plus a cellar that had an entrance inside the home. Helena was elated and proud of her home. She kept it spotless and enjoyed entertaining neighbors and relatives there.

Michael had arranged for a well to be dug before the first winter the family lived on the farm. When the desired water level was reached, a wooden crib Michael had built was lowered into the well. The cover for the well consisted of wooden boards placed loosely over the top of the crib, about two feet above the ground. To obtain water, the boards were manually removed, and a pail attached to a rope was lowered to the water level. The pail was flipped using the rope, filling the pail with water. Then the rope and pail of water were drawn up by hand. This was a difficult and unsafe procedure, especially for the children.

Helena pleaded with Michael to have a water pump installed in the well. Michael felt it would be difficult to maintain a pump, particularly during the winter months, and chose not to have it done. During the winter months, the water that spilled over froze into ice, making it very treacherous around the well. Larger quantities of water were required for the cattle as the stream was frozen during the winter. Water in the water troughs had to be replenished when the cattle were outside. It became very dangerous for the individual drawing the water, most particularly when the cattle were thirsty. They would come running for a drink, pushing aside anything that was in their way.

One spring day, while the children were at school, Michael was at the well drawing water for the cattle. A couple of piglets came running from the barn area to the open well as Michael was emptying a pail of water in the trough for the cattle. One of the piglets fell into the well. Michael called for Helena. She quickly came to the well from the house, got the cattle and other piglet into the barn area. The piglet in the well was alive, trying to stay afloat. You could hear the squealing noise coming from the well.

A ladder had been built on one side of the crib in the well. Michael climbed down this ladder and got a hold of the piglet by an ear with one hand, while hanging on to the ladder with his other hand. He pulled the piglet closer to him and was able to hold on to the piglet by wrapping his arm around the piglet's abdomen. Michael did not have enough strength to climb back up the ladder while holding on to the squirming piglet. Helena was beside herself, not knowing what she should do to help Michael. She was worried that he would fall off the ladder, into the water. The water was very cold and Michael would have difficulty surviving in it for very long, even though he was a good swimmer.

During this crisis, a neighbor, Nick Adams, happened to drop by. He was on his way to town and wanted to know if Michael and Helena needed anything from the store. Helena shouted, "We need help in the well. Michael and a young pig are down there." Nick quickly ran to the area, kneeled down in front of the well opening, and looked down into the well. He took the rope off the water pail, lowered it into the well to Michael and suggested Michael tie the rope around the abdomen of the piglet. Nick would try to pull the piglet up slowly while Michael kept control of the rope and piglet during his climb up the ladder and out of the well. They were successful. After a few minutes, which seemed much longer to Helena, Michael reached the well opening, holding on to the piglet, his body a little wet and chilled, but he was in good spirits. Helena suggested they have a cup of hot tea to warm up and get Michael into some dry clothes. A lot of discussion took place over tea and cookies. Michael commented on the knot he used in tying the rope around the piglet, it was one he used frequently while working on the ship.

Helena and Michael were most appreciative for Nick's assistance in this successful endeavor. However, the water in the well was contaminated and would have to be removed manually—by rope and pail. Nick stayed on and helped Michael with this procedure, which was time-consuming and laborious. The next day, the water level in the well returned and was considered free from contamination, safe again for household use.

This crisis that Michael experienced was very traumatic for him and his family. He was finally convinced that the well, without a pump was a hazard to the family. He purchased a pump and had it installed. Helena was pleased with this improvement. She would have appreciated having the pump when the well was originally installed, but better late than never, she said to herself as she envisioned the pleasures they would all have using this luxury facility.

FORTY-THREE

Emily's thoughts fluttered over her nursing student experiences and life in the residence with all the other students. She frequently socialized with the students, both outside and within. Emily was able to buy her uniforms, cape and books for nursing with the money she had earned from teaching, but she had very little money left for necessities during the three-year period. One way Emily learned she could obtain some money was to collect pop and chocolate milk bottles around the hospital premises and sell them at a nearby store. Emily was most thankful to the hospital for this availability and most grateful to the patients for this benefit.

Emily looked forward to receiving newsy letters from her mother. It made her feel really good. She loved hearing about all of her family and their activities. Most of the family members had left home, were educated or becoming educated on their own initiative, with support from Helena. Helena wrote letters to each one of her children and tried to make each visit at home a special occasion, preparing their food preferences.

Emily remembered so vividly her trips home from Winnipeg by bus each year during her three-week vacation period at nursing school. After a ten-hour bus ride, Emily had to walk two miles on a dirt road to her parent's home on the farm. She prayed that it would not rain before and during her walk from the bus because the road would become very muddy and difficult to walk on, especially when one was carrying a heavy suitcase. Going home was exciting and she could hardly wait to see her parents and siblings.

Emily did not get much sleep the first night visiting at home. Everyone was anxious to talk to her, asking many questions. She, in turn, was anxious to hear about their activities. Emily and her sisters slept together on a pullout bed in the living room and a mattress on the floor close by. They laughed and talked until the wee hours of the morning. They were happy, memorable occasions.

Emily looked back at her first three-week vacation at home. Helena had arranged for a family portrait to be taken on a Saturday morning in the town twenty miles away. Helena had saved some funds for this purpose when working in the sewing factory. The problem was, having everyone home together when the photographer was available.

It was a hectic Saturday morning as each family member prepared for this photo shoot. There was only one large mirror in the home and each person hogged this mirror, trying to do wonders with what they had. Sophie kept changing her hairstyle, requiring more time at the mirror. Finally Helena spoke in a loud voice that it was time to leave. She did not want to lose her appointment with the photographer. Following much pushing and discussion as to which sibling had the next turn at the mirror; everyone headed for the truck, their transportation vehicle.

Andrew suggested the siblings arrange themselves on the back of the half-ton truck, sitting on the floor, on an old worn out blanket. Michael drove along the lane to the road. Prior to reaching the gate, the back wheels of the truck became deeply immersed in mud from the rainfall that took place during the night. Michael suggested the siblings all push from the back of the truck. They all jumped out of the truck and began pushing as hard as they could. They were successful in this endeavor, but there were a few problems. Each one had mud splattered on their good dress clothes, face and hair, plus their shoes were muddy and soaking wet. How does one continue with this very important family project? The only dress clothing each sibling had was presently worn. After much discussion, Rosie suggested they all continue their journey to the studio. Having a family picture was very important to Helena. The siblings returned to the back of the truck, cuddled in close to each other to protect their wet bodies from the cool wind and started singing to keep their minds off all of their discomforts.

At the studio, the photographer aligned everyone in a group. From under the black hood over the camera, he hollered, "Smile!" No one seemed interested in smiling. The riders in the back of the truck were wind-blown plus their feet and clothing were wet. The photographer came out from under the black hood with a concerned look on his face and was about to speak again when Alex saved the moment. He farted out, releasing some bowel sounds (gas) in the quiet atmosphere and triggering smiles and laughter from each one. A portrait of a happy family was the outcome. Surprisingly, the mud on the clothing did not show up in the photograph.

RETIREMENT

PART THREE
The Golden Years and the Rewards

MICHAEL and HELENA

FORTY-FOUR

Each of Michael and Helena's children became educated and moved into occupations of their choosing. Andrew chose farming and the political field. He was a big asset to the community. Alex chose the real estate venture, becoming very successful at it. Rosie continued with her flair for teaching. Sophie studied and worked in the business field, gradually developing and managing her own ladies clothing store. Emily had a long career in nursing administration. Jane also graduated in nursing. After several years of working in the nursing field, she decided to apply for law school and was accepted. Jane had an extremely heavy schedule, attending classes and working in nursing on a part-time basis to pay for her education. She succeeded and joined a small law firm in Dauphin. Shortly after the youngest sibling left the home, Michael decided to venture out of farming and obtain employment in Winnipeg. He really did not enjoy struggling with the farm issues, unable to make ends meet most years. Michael applied for a maintenance job with the post office and was immediately hired. Helena was very pleased. They were also accepted in a seniors' low-rental apartment building, had a comfortable dwelling and were happy with the changes in their lives. Their plan was to return to the country where they lived, after Michael would have retired from the post office job and received his old-age pension. All of this did take place.

Following Michael's retirement, Michael and Helena sold

their farm and built a small home in the country on an acre of land, close to where they used to live. Their home was close to Rosie and Andrew and their families, providing many happy get—togethers. Michael planted many trees for wind protection, also fruit trees. This was a change from cutting down trees in the past. He cultivated an area for a vegetable garden and large lawn. Helena planted and maintained a large garden. The one-acre of property was like a park, loved and enjoyed by everyone who paid them a visit. Michael and Helena seemed at peace at last, enjoying their life in retirement with trees, beautiful flowers, fruits, a lawn to play on with the grandchildren, plus a garden with sufficient vegetables to give to family and friends when they visited. Michael built a couple of benches at the lawn. Helena loved to utilize this area for her mid-meal snacks, particularly when she had family or friends visiting. To Michael and Helena, having a lawn was a luxury, a waste of good soil. They were proud to be able to have the lawn as part of their residence. At long last, Michael and Helena were living comfortably and did not have to struggle to make ends meet. There was always food available whenever anyone visited and Helena was delighted to prepare a meal or a snack at anytime. She was proud to share her specialty dishes and desserts.

Helena was ecstatic when she received her first old-age pension check. She immediately bought gifts for each of her grandchildren. Her thoughts kept focusing on how wonderful it was going to be to have her very own money to spend. Throughout her life, Helena did not have money to spend on herself or what she would have liked for the family. She constantly worked to try to help in providing the necessities for the family. This was not always accomplished to her desire.

Helena saved a little of the pension money each month and wanted she and Michael to spend this money each year, visiting one of their children who lived far off. It would give them an opportunity to spend time with each family plus enjoy different geographic areas and new experiences. Michael agreed to a family visit each year for the first two years, and then decided he no longer had an interest in travel. His desire was to remain at home where he was most comfortable. When Helena approached Michael regarding future visits, he declined. Helena decided to venture out on her own and each year she looked forward to visiting with a family for several weeks. While on visit, she also kept busy baking, cooking, and making special Ukrainian dishes. Every one looked forward to her visit. The children of each family loved perogies and tried to include their friends for a feast, when they knew Grandma was making them. Helena used her sewing skills, making gifts of clothing for the grandchildren before her arrival, plus offering to mend or alter any needed clothing articles. Helena also crocheted doilies, an Afghan and a tablecloth for each daughter, daughter-in-law, and granddaughter. The finished work was very beautiful and very much appreciated. Helena was hoping her daughters or granddaughters would take an interest in crocheting and tried to encourage them, but she was not successful. They all seemed taken up with many other interests.

While Helena was away, Rosie kept close contact with Michael. They spent a great deal of time together. Rosie wanted to make sure Michael's diet was adequate. She cooked special casserole dishes for him and baked his favorite cookies. Michael very much enjoyed this special attention. During one of these visits in 1970, Michael noticed Rosie put her hand to her chest periodically while they were conversing. She also seemed very tired. Rosie called Michael the next day, stating she thought she had the flu and would not be seeing him for a few days. Helena was arriving home in two days so they would get together sometime following her mother's arrival.

When Helena arrived home, Michael expressed his concerns regarding Rosie. Helena immediately called Rosie and had a chat with her. Rosie indicated she really felt tired the last couple weeks. She felt as though she had a touch of flu. However, she was resting a lot and felt a little improvement. Helena asked Rosie if she had cough or pain in her chest. Rosie answered she sometimes felt heaviness in her chest. She saw her doctor the day before and he examined her. Her doctor did not identify a problem but suggested she have some diagnostic work, if she was not improving in a few days.

Helena felt a concern regarding Rosie's health situation. Rosie had indicated to her mother at one time that she was considering giving up square dancing. It seemed to take her a couple days to recuperate from an evening of square dancing. Helena went to bed with concerned thoughts about Rosie, having some difficulty falling asleep. She did doze off in the early hours of the morning but was awakened around 6:00 A.M. by the neighbor's dog barking. Helena got out of bed, as she was anxious to start the day and talk to Rosie.

Helena and Michael were finishing their breakfast at 7:00 A.M. when they heard a car driving in their yard. They both wondered who would be calling on them so early in the morning. Michael looked out the window and saw Andrew walking to the door. He had a very concerned look on his face. Michael's immediate thought was that there were some farming problems.

"Andrew, what are you doing here so early in the morning? Would you like some breakfast?" asked Helena.

"I have some bad news for you and I do not know how to tell you. Rosie was taken to the hospital during the night with chest pain. She died shortly after the ambulance got her there," Andrew quickly informed them. He knew how traumatic it would be for Michael and Helena to receive this unbelievable news. They were devastated.

"How could this happen when the doctor is close by and Rosie saw the doctor two days ago? There must be a mistake, Andrew, tell me this is not true, Helena hollered out as she sobbed. We lost our first child because there was not a doctor available to us, but with Rosie, there was a doctor. What caused her to die so quickly?"

"The doctor said she had a real bad heart attack", replied Andrew.

"How could she have a real bad heart attack when she was so young? continued Helena as she wept bitterly. Her poor husband and children, how will they manage without her? She was too young to die, too young. I wish God had taken me instead of Rosie. I really do. I cannot see our life without Rosie."

Michael did not say anything while Helena and Andrew were conversing. He was stunned and very deep in thought, thinking back to the most recent enjoyable times he had with Rosie visiting him when Helena was away. Michael realized this was a traumatic disaster for the whole family He tried consoling Helena by telling her they needed to keep up their courage. Rosie's family would really need their help and support. It would be very difficult, but very necessary.

This crisis had a big impact on Michael and Helena as well as on Rosie's family. Helena was used to talking to Rosie on a daily basis, if they were not seeing each other. Helena felt very lost and lonely, frequently questioning herself if she was going to be able to cope. With other family members visiting more frequently, she gradually put her life together by helping and supporting the very needy at this time: Rosie's children. Helena felt close to Rosie when communicating with Rosie's children. She told them about specific incidents involving their mother. The younger children were anxious to hear and learn more about their mother, as they grew older. Helena was happy to answer as many questions as she could about their mother. She also loved to cook and bake for the children. This relationship and time together made Helena feel so much better, she felt she was contributing.

FORTY-FIVE

During the latter years of Helena's life, Emily and her husband were living in Florida as retirees. Helena showed an interest in visiting them in Florida but was unable to travel that distance on her own. Her nephew, Orest, and his wife, were planning a trip to Florida one winter, and invited Helena to travel with them. This was the most wonderful experience for Helena and Emily.

When Helena arrived at the Southwest Florida airport, she could not believe what she was seeing: all the flowers, greenery, and no snow in February. It was a reality she had not experienced in the winter months before. Helena wished Michael had come with her to see Florida. It was so different; many palm trees, sand beaches. People were lying on the beach, some at the poolside. Helena was not used to seeing people sitting in the sun, doing nothing. She worked in her garden in the sun. When sitting, she was either having a cup of tea, chatting, or working on a useful craft. These people were lying or sitting with no activity. It was a totally different lifestyle.

Helena enjoyed the car trips each day, seeing different places around Naples. Having lunch at a restaurant was new to her. Condominiums were new to her. Helena could not understand why people would want to live on the beach and look at water. Her vision of beauty was looking at trees or a garden, watching their growth. However, after a few days, Emily noticed her mother periodically sitting restfully on the balcony, watching the boats and activity on the beach.

This was a true vacation for Helena. She offered to help clean up after meals and place the dishes in the dishwasher, but did not get involved in cooking or any special projects. Emily was thrilled to see her mother relaxed and enjoying being catered to, without too much encouragement. Helena enjoyed trying new foods and showing an interest in them.

On the morning before the day of Helena's departure, Helena was packing while Emily prepared lunch. While eating lunch, Helena informed Emily that she had one dress she had not worn while visiting. She had brought a different dress for each day but the dress she had not worn was kind of special. Emily indicated they were having a special dinner that evening and she would look great wearing her special dress for dinner. Helena was pleased with this response.

When Helena arrived at the dinner table, she felt very proud and looked very elegant in her special, blue-flowered dress, white shoes, and her very special pearl necklace. Helena had reached her senior years graciously, respecting her position as a role model for her family. She did gradually adapt to wearing slacks, but did not adapt to wearing shorts.

Emily kissed her mother as she was seated at the table, stating she would like to express a special prayer before dinner. After everyone was seated, Emily suggested they all hold hands and bow their heads.

"You have been an inspiration to so many of us, Mom. Your never-ending strength and perseverance gave me the courage and support to say to myself so many times . . . Of course you can do it! . . . and I did! You were always there for me; that is why I was successful. Thank you so very much, Mom!"

Helena was really elated with this recognition. She shed a few tears as she slowly responded, "I only did what I thought I was supposed to do. I wanted so much for my family to have a good life, and they did, even though some had shorter lives. The loss of Bohdan made me aware of the need for medical attention when a child is ill. When Rosie was a baby and had pneumonia, like Bohdan did, I was forceful in having her treated by a doctor and she improved. I am so happy we were able to provide antibiotics for Rosie. All of our children had the freedom to continue their education and were successful. I feel it was a big accomplishment, and am so very proud of their achievements. Michael and I each receive a monthly government pension, plus Michael receives a monthly pension from his work at the post office. We each receive free health care, including prescription drugs that are frequently needed in senior years. In my opinion we are very comfortable and could not wish for anything more. Everyone does not get to travel, but we have been able to do some traveling, visiting our children. Our country, Canada, has been good to us, helping us become independent in our senior years. Orest, you and your family have also been very good to us and I want to thank you. We all had some rough times over the years, but we also had so many good times. I have many beautiful memories."

Michael and Helena later gave up their home in the country and moved to an apartment for senior citizens in town. They had difficulty managing without indoor bathroom facilities in their home in the country, particularly during the winter months. Family members were concerned for them as there were very few neighbors around their home. Most of the neighbors were elderly and had relocated elsewhere.

Michael had difficulty adapting to apartment living. He felt uncomfortable in a home and property that he did not own. His country home was his very own, including the property, and that meant so much to him. After all, he worked most of his life to be a landowner. That was the reason his father and family became settlers in this country. Michael frequently reminded Helena and family members of his negative feelings for their present lifestyle. Michael felt he had betrayed his dad by giving up his own land. Helena enjoyed maintaining the apartment, using the more modern facilities. It was a little more crowded when family members came for visits but that situation did not reduce the frequency of their visits. Helena enjoyed preparing for each one.

Following Michael's death, Helena's health became a problem, requiring more personalized care. At first, she struggled with the fact that she was no longer a caregiver; she was receiving care instead. Gradually Helena warmed up to the staff, appreciating and looking forward to the time they were spending with her. She spoke highly of them to her family.

On the flight to Minneapolis, the pilot was preparing for landing. He began making announcements on the PA system. Emily faintly heard something about Minneapolis in the background. She felt someone's hand on her shoulder and realized it was the flight attendant asking her to place her seat upright for landing. It took Helena a few minutes to realize where she was and what was happening in her life.

When Emily entered Gate 29 at the Minneapolis Airport, she could see her sister Sophie sitting in a far seat near a window, reading the newspaper. Emily was looking forward to the two-hour wait they had before leaving for Winnipeg. This time together would be beneficial to both of them, she thought. Flying time from Minneapolis to Winnipeg would take one hour. The bus ride from Winnipeg to their parents' hometown was about eight hours, providing they made the next bus connection and fewer stops along the way. Just as Emily reached Sophie and greeted her with a big hug, she felt her mother's spirit reaching out to her. It was a wonderful feeling. She wondered if Sophie could also feel their mother. Helena had always been there for her family, caring, supporting, communicating, providing, and always loving them. Emily was not surprised to have her mother continue in this role, after her death. As far as Emily was concerned, Helena would never give up her responsibilities. Maybe she would join the family in spirit as their guardian angel. Emily could not help but question her belief. She thought about asking Sophie if she believed in guardian angels. Would Emily continue in this belief if Sophie responded negatively? Emily recalled a statement made by her mother recently, *Do not ask the question because you may not always like the answer.* Yes, thought Emily, I am not going to ask this question. *You have always been and will always be my guardian angel, Mom. Hopefully, your spirit will continue in guiding me forever. Thank you so very much, Mom!*

MOM

You taught us to think our own thoughts
And to follow our own dreams,
To be proud of our achievements
And accepting of our mistakes,
To find peace in each sunset
And joy in each sunrise . . .
To love life . . .

Thank you, Mom . . . EDE

HELENA:
A WOMAN OF
SUBSTANCE

As a child you came to a promised land
A land of toil and wooded terrain
With your head held high you persevered
Managed the stress and strain
The stress of work, a life of hope
You challenged from day to day
The strain of responsibility advanced your years
There was so little time for relaxation and play
We love you, Mom, for all you have done
In guiding us through the years
The years of sharing, loving and support
Prepared us for the unknown fears
Fears of life when you are all alone
Reduce when you know someone will care
Your strength gave a substance of achievement to all
We thank you so very much for our share

DAD

Having lived with the spirit of Nature;
Has encouraged in us an awareness that
There is a religion in everything around us . . .
A calm and holy religion in all things of Nature;
It can uplift the spirit within us until it is strong
Enough to overlook the shadows in our lives,
And can open to us a world of spiritual beauty
And holiness . . . bringing us peace!

Thank you, Dad . . . EDE

MICHAEL:
A MAN OF PHILOSOPHY

Your life has been a contest, Dad
With a win or lose to bear
From cordwood cutting to seamanship
Experiences were not rare
The business world you challenged
With your philosophical mind
You brought a flare of dignity
To all surrounding mankind
Then on to a world of mining
You battled the underground
Handled the dangers courageously
Without an injury to be found
Farming then became a way of life
For many tough years to come
Followed by a stint with the government
Until you acquired a financial sum
Gave up the structured workforce
To live the life you loved so much
Engrossed in nature's world outdoors
You provided the expert touch
Built a park around your home
Grew fruit and vegetables to share
With family members as they came

To visit in the clean, fresh air
Yes, life has been a contest, Dad
And you a winner all the way
You taught each of us the love of life
And the richness in each day

Life excels beauty
  Life inspires hope
    Life promotes happiness
      Life can be so very rewarding

AUTHOR'S BIOGRAPHY

M ary Kolisnyk Spry-Myers was born and grew up in the countryside of Manitoba, Canada. Mary found her visits to her grandparents very enjoyable, giving her the opportunity to experience Ukrainian culture. She also enjoyed listening to her grandparents and parents talk about their life in Ukraine, their experiences in immigrating to Canada, and their life in Canada as new settlers. These experiences inspired Mary to write a historical fiction novel,

Beyond the Wilds, Helena's Pursuit of Freedom

Mary hopes that her readers, especially Ukrainian and those of other origins, will be inspired in looking back to their ancestral roots and in developing their knowledge of their family culture and heritage.

Mary presently lives in Naples, Florida, with her husband, Gordon Myers. Her published works include a children's book, *A Hole in the Sky*, and a cassette of poems with background music, *A Reflection of Life's Seasons*.

BVG